TWO TIMES A VICTIM

The woman who'd bought the drug lay sprawled on the deck, faceup. The man pulled his knife. He knelt beside her, looked down at her, surprised because her face wasn't as dirty as most users. She hadn't been living this life very long.

"Too bad," said the man. "You should have stayed home."

He pressed the tip of his knife against her stomach and slowly increased the pressure until it cut through the clothing. He pushed harder and felt the blade slip easily into her body. . . .

STAR PRECINCT
INSIDE JOB

KEVIN RANDLE
AND
RICHARD DRISCOLL

ACE BOOKS, NEW YORK

This book is an Ace original edition,
and has never been previously published.

INSIDE JOB

An Ace Book / published by arrangement with
the authors

PRINTING HISTORY
Ace edition / December 1992

All rights reserved.
Copyright © 1992 by Kevin Randle and Richard Driscoll.
Cover art by Jean Pierre Targete.
This book may not be reproduced in whole or in part,
by mimeograph or any other means, without permission.
For information address: The Berkley Publishing Group,
200 Madison Avenue, New York, New York 10016.

ISBN: 0-441-78270-1

Ace Books are published by The Berkley Publishing Group,
200 Madison Avenue, New York, New York 10016.
The name "ACE" and the "A" logo
are trademarks belonging to Charter Communications, Inc.

PRINTED IN THE UNITED STATES OF AMERICA
10 9 8 7 6 5 4 3 2 1

Prologue | A Crack in Time

They were in the dark reaches of the precinct ship, near the bottom where the engines were housed and the generating stations for the electrical power were placed. It was dim, the light filtering down from the catwalks and passageways above, it was warm because of the heat generated by the engines, and it was damp because of the filtration systems and collection reservoirs. At times, if the precinct was running at full speed, and if the various components of the precinct were functioning at full or near full capacity, it could be oppressive hidden away down there.

They sat in a loose circle, two of the men leaning against bulkheads while a woman sat in the center. She stuffed the rocklike drug into the tip of a pipe, held a lighter to it, then inhaled rapidly, sucking the fumes deep into her lungs. Finished for the moment, she passed the pipe to the woman closest to her and then laid back, on the desk, her eyes closed.

The group was ragged; the clothes, old and dirty. They wore a mixture of styles and garments and mismatched shoes. One woman wore little more than what was necessary for modesty, her bare skin smudged with dirt and grease. Another was covered from her throat to her ankles though her feet were bare. A man wore a pair of pants with one leg missing, a shirt with a sleeve gone, and an old knit cap that was so dirty that no one knew what color it had been originally.

"Give me!" said a man, holding out his hand. "Give me." He took the pipe, put it between his lips, held the lighter up, and sucked deeply. The expression on his face, first one of pain and anxiety, changed slowly until he was so relaxed that the woman beside him had to take the drug pipe from his slack fingers.

In minutes, the drug was gone but the people had all taken one hit from it. They were sprawled on the deck and slumped against the bulkheads, grinning widely but unable to move quickly or with coordination. The things they saw, their minds fogged by the drug, might have been real, might have been illusion, or might have been a combination of both. They didn't know and didn't care. They had been lifted from the deck and swept up with euphoria, happy to be there and happy to have found a little drug to improve the day.

Slowly, carefully, a man stood, sweat pouring from his face and soaking his clothes. With great care, he unbuttoned his shirt and slipped it off, dropping it to the deck. He peeled himself out of his clothes until he stood only in his hole-filled socks, stained underpants, and ripped T-shirt. Then he closed his eyes, tilted his head back, and held out his arms as if he expected to receive a gift from the gods.

A hatchway cracked and was forced open, spilling bright light from the companionway. Caught in the light were half the men and women. Only one bothered to hold up a hand to shield her eyes but she didn't ask what was happening. At the moment she didn't care.

"Told you," said one of the shapes that stepped into the hatchway, blocking some of the light. "I told you they would be here and that they would be so strung out that they wouldn't even move."

"Shit, it smells in here."

"It's them. Never wash. Never change clothes. Just sit around drifting on high until they crash. Fuck 'em."

One of the men stepped inside and walked to the woman sprawled at the center of the circle. He crouched, grabbed a handful of her tangled and dirty hair, and lifted her head so that he could look at her face. Her eyes were half-closed and her features slack.

"Doesn't have a clue about what's going on. Not a fucking clue."

The other stepped closer and looked down. "She'd be kind of pretty if she'd clean up."

"Too skinny. Way too skinny. Need to get some food into her first." He let her head fall back to the deck with an audible clunk. Slipping a knife from his boot, he held it up, in front of her face but she didn't seem to recognize it as a weapon.

"Do it," said his partner. "Cut her."

The man sliced the buttons from her shirt and pulled it open exposing her bare chest. He touched the point of the knife just above her belly button and drew it toward him, cutting her, though not deeply. A bright crimson line appeared as the blood began to flow. She didn't react. It was as if she were completely unaware.

"Oh, yeah. They're out of it." The second intruder jerked a man to his feet, pushed him back so that he was leaning against the wall. "Watch." Taking his own knife, he plunged it into the stomach of the drugged man. He ripped it out, dripping blood, and let go of the victim. Without bothering to try to stop the blood, without even putting a hand to the wound, the man slipped to the floor, still grinning happily.

"Fucker's dying and doesn't even know it."

The first man still crouched over the woman. He touched a finger to the blood on her chest and then drew a line connecting her nipples. Then, suddenly, he stabbed down, into her body, the knife slicing through the soft skin and penetrating her chest. Blood fountained, splattering the desk and bulkhead and some of the others. No one said a word.

The odor of hot copper filled the confined space as blood flowed and pooled under the first two victims. But now the men were caught in the blood lust. They wanted to see more of it, they needed to see it splattering, and they had to kill the last of the drug users to assure that no one was conscious enough to provide a description of the killers.

The two men worked quickly, slashing, stabbing, cutting, and killing. The super-sharp knives, created from tempered glass because they could take a sharper edge, cut with nearly no pain. None of the people reacted as the knives sliced into them. None of them seemed aware that they were being killed.

Finally, the last of the victims was dead, her blood puddling under her body. The man stood, his dripping knife held in his left hand. He looked down at the dead woman, her clothing soaked in blood.

"That'll stop them now."

"We'd better get the hell out of here."

"Yeah." He surveyed the scene a final time. Bodies slumped against the bulkhead or sprawled on the floor, hot copper and bowel filling the air. He wiped the sweat from his face and then studied his own hands, covered in blood. "We're going to have to be careful. We don't want to be seen now."

"Showers in the lower crew rest compartment. Nobody uses them except during maintenance of the engine areas."

"Good. Let's get out of here." He moved to the hatch and peeked out into the corridor. There were no people in it and the single surveillance camera that had been installed so long ago had been ripped out by the druggies. He stepped out and hurried from the scene of the crime. Without looking back, he knew his partner was there.

Together they hurried along the passageway, avoiding the open areas, until they reached the rear crew shower. Without a word, they entered and began to destroy the evidence of the crime. In just over ten minutes they would be back on the upper levels and no one would be the wiser.

1 | Boring Holes in the Sky

Duty on the precinct as it traveled among the star systems that made up its patrol zone was not the most exciting time for anyone. Routine work, overlooked in the process of finishing the job, now had to be completed. Reports had to be filled out, reviewed by the brass, and filed with the district headquarters, now more than forty light-years away. Just because it was that far away didn't mean that it didn't keep close tabs on what had once been called paperwork or busy work and which made up the bulk of the effort exhibited by the Star Cops.

Lieutenant Richard Brackett sat at the keyboard and looked at the blank screen in front of him. In the old days enterprising cops had programmed games of skill and intelligence into the computer so that a man who couldn't get started on the overdue report would have something to do. Now, those programs had been wiped out and there was one computer expert whose job it was to make sure that no other games were added, though the memory for them existed.

Brackett, who had started life as a con man, sometimes wished that he'd never switched sides. Though police work teased the brain in the same fashion that inventing the con did, the problem revolved around the reports. He didn't like sitting there constructing a report to be read by someone he didn't know about a case that he had already finished. He wanted to get on to the next job.

Brackett knew that he was going to have to start the report because it was due in Captain Carnes's office soon so that Carnes could review it before it was dispatched. But Brackett just couldn't get started. He couldn't think of the first words to write, couldn't think of a good structure for the report, and would rather have scraped rust on the outside of the precinct, had the precinct been built of materials that would rust, or if rust could form in space.

He pushed back against his chair until he was an arm's length from the computer and stared at the flashing cursor that seemed to be berating him for his failure to begin his work.

There was a tap at the bulkhead and Brackett rolled his eyes upward, as if to thank God that someone had arrived to rescue him from the challenge. He turned and spotted Sergeant Jennifer Daily standing there, leaning around the corner, one hand up on the bulkhead.

"You busy?" she asked.

"Not really. What can I do for you?"

She seemed to pull herself around the corner and then entered, dropping into the only other chair. She was a very pretty redhead assigned to the 107th because of her degrees in sociology and psychology and because Carnes thought that good police work included a large helping of sociology and psychology.

Daily was wearing her police uniform, complete with leather belt, handcuff case, and drill baton. She sat down, tugged at the hem of her narrow skirt, and then crossed her legs slowly.

"Can you get me off the rotation for radio supervisor?"

Brackett grinned, thinking of the report that he couldn't write, and wished that lieutenants were assigned the role of radio supervisor. Unfortunately there was a captain who ran communications, three lieutenants who were assigned, and then a rotating list of sergeants, dragged in so that they would be exposed to the procedures. It was thought of as a career-developing move.

He began with the standard speech but she put up a hand. "It's boring. Important messages, computer bubbles, and files are couriered out and do not move through our end of communications. Unless we're close to a planet and on assignment, there is nothing happening there. Radio waves travel only at the speed of light."

"You're filling squares so that when you march in front of the promotion board, they'll see that you've been exposed to various aspects of the job."

"Loot, there is nothing to do. I sit there for eight hours with nothing to do. I've got the radio operators sitting there playing games because the radios are useless."

"I understand, but we've all had to do it."

"I don't care about the work. I'm happy to do it, but we don't have any. None. And the day-watch lieutenant is a little . . . no, make that a big asshole."

"He is your temporary supervisor."

"I'm not learning anything there. I'm wasting my time. I could be doing something else, something more useful. I know that you have reports to get filed. I could help there."

Brackett leaned rearward in his chair, hooking an elbow over the back, and remembered that Daily spent her off-duty hours hunched over a computer working on a video to be produced for the entertainment of the masses. If she was comfortable with words, if she enjoyed writing, then she might have given him the answer to his problem.

"Have you handled communications before?"

"Sure. Couple of times. Once we were working the Argyle case and I was elevated into one of the lieutenant's positions when he took sick. I've filled that block."

"Okay," said Brackett, "let me talk to our captain and see what I can work out. You off duty now?"

"Just came off."

Brackett looked at the chronometer just above his computer. "Me too." He reached around, thinking that he would save the day's production, but there was nothing to save. He'd managed to waste the entire shift.

"We could catch a drink at the Off-Duty," said Daily. "I could use a little noise and diversion."

Brackett shut down his computer and watched the cursor die quietly. He stood up and said, "You'll buy the first round?"

"Sure."

They walked out together but Brackett stopped at the admin desk. The sergeant there, an old man with most of an arm missing, was using an artificial hand to type codes into a computer. The arm had failed to regenerate properly due to excessive nerve and brain damage. The doctors had been unable to stimulate new growth.

"Checking out. If the captain wants me, I'll be in the Off-Duty for a while and then back to my cabin."

"Yes, sir. Captain asked about the progress of your report." The sergeant stared up, as if to say that he knew that no progress had been made. Computers allowed those with the proper codes to spy on everything.

"He'll have it tomorrow afternoon."

Raising an eyebrow, the sergeant said, "Yes, sir. Tomorrow."

As they left, entering a long, narrow corridor that was still brightly lighted, Daily asked, "What was all that?"

"Having a little difficulty in getting my reports written for the brass."

She grinned broadly and said, "I thought you caved in on my request a little too easily. Now I understand why."

They reached the lift and stopped. Brackett touched the key pad and a moment later the door slid open. They took it down to the lower deck and then exited.

In that corridor, the lighting was subdued. It was a recreational and retail level, where bars, gyms, gaming house, shops, and stores were located. Neon, announcing the services or merchandise available, twinkled on the bulkheads close to the hatches. The corridor was filled with people, looking as if they were in a mall back on Earth. The cadence was slow, almost hypnotic, as the people strolled.

There was a single blast of noise from the Off-Duty. It was the loudest, most crowded bar on the level. It catered to the Star Cops, to those in the support functions for them and the groupies, both male and female, who wanted to get close to the cops. Its parallel in a different time would have been the fighter pilot clubs on old Earth.

"We're not going to do much talking in there," said Daily as another rock tune from the ancient past began to pound.

"No, but we can get something to drink," said Brackett. "Right now I feel like I've been in the desert for a week. I need something to drink."

He shouldered his way in, looking at the crowd pressed against the bar. Many of them wore uniforms showing they were either coming off work or about to go to it. A half-dozen men and women worked behind the bar, running from customer to customer, pouring booze into small glasses or filling tankards with beer.

Brackett, with Daily following, pushed toward the rear where the tables and booths were. The crowd thinned slightly, once they were past the dance floor bathed in a bright orange light. Brackett spotted two men vacating a booth and rushed forward, claiming it before anyone else could react.

When Daily joined him, she asked, "How do you always luck out?"

"I live right, eat my vegetables, and believe in a benevolent supreme being."

"Sure."

The waitress, a long, skinny robot of metal, plastic, and lights, appeared, seemed to bow its head, and asked, "What is your desire?"

"Beer," said Brackett.

"Two," said Daily.

The waitress turned, hesitated, and then faced them, the two mugs on a tray held out in front. Brackett grabbed the mugs and set one in front of Daily as the waitress, having coded Brackett's face into her memory, disappeared.

Daily took a drink, wiped her lips with the back of her hand, and said, "So you're going to have me write the report, aren't you, Loot?"

"You're the one always bragging about your creative talent. Why shouldn't I make use of it?"

"And this will get me off the radio watch?"

"Right."

"Then I have no trouble with it." She took another pull at the beer, watching Brackett over the top of the mug. When he glanced up into her face, she lowered her eyes.

At that moment something changed in the booth. Both of them felt it and both were surprised by it. They were suddenly aware of each other as people and not police officers. Had the lighting been better, and had the colors been anything other than reds and oranges, Daily knew that Brackett would see that she was blushing. Her face was as hot as fire and she knew exactly what it meant.

Brackett, to conceal his discomfort, took a long drink, and then twisted around so that he was no longer facing her. He scanned the crowd, searching for anything to break the moment, to cut the tension, but it didn't seem that anyone was going to rescue him.

Then, as if he'd been summoned, Obo appeared. He stood in the hatch of the Off-Duty, towering over the humans, scanning the crowd. The red and orange lights reflected from him, giving his normally blue skin a bizarre and sickening color.

Brackett rose slightly and raised a hand. Obo spotted it and began to work his way through the crowd, moving with a grace that belied his size. He reached the booth but made no move to sit down.

"Captain is looking for you," he said without preamble.

Brackett glanced up at him and nodded, thinking that Obo's command of the English language had improved greatly. "Say what he wanted?"

"Just said to locate you and have you report to him."

"Probably because you didn't finish your reports," said Daily helpfully.

"I doubt the captain would go out of his way to summon me because of that."

"Sure he would," said Daily happily. "The captain would do anything he thought would irritate you. That is his mission in life. Make things as miserable for the rest of us as he can. Now that you've left the office, he wants to summon you so that he ruins your off-duty time."

"Captain said to hurry," said Obo.

Brackett picked up his beer and drained it quickly and then regretted that. Spikes slammed into his head from drinking it too fast. He closed his eyes momentarily.

"Captain's down near the engineering plants."

"What?"

"Lower levels. Said to get there as quickly as possible."

Brackett touched his lips with the back of his hand and then looked at Daily. "You want to come?"

"And see Carnes? Not likely."

Brackett slipped to the left and stood. "Might be interesting if Carnes is down in engineering."

"Okay," said Daily. "You've convinced me."

2 | Everyone Has to Be Somewhere

The sergeant had led Carnes down to the lower levels where the captain never ventured. His existence belonged on the upper levels, away from the heat and noise of the engines and power plants that fueled the needs of the precinct. There were maintenance crews, support personnel, and various workers whose job it was to maintain the ship and to keep it functioning. Carnes had no desire to know how it was done. He didn't care about the people who were responsible for it. All he wanted was for the power to be there when he wanted it, for his equipment to function properly when he needed it, and for those who performed those tasks to stay out of his way and out of his sight.

Carnes was a career police officer who had risen through the ranks, not because he was an investigative genius or because of his spectacular arrest record. He rose because his father had been an inspector and his grandfather had been one of the first men assigned to the 107th. And he rose because his aunt, his father's sister, had commanded the precinct for fifteen years. When the adults had risen so high, it was impossible for the children not to do well. There were so many who would cover for them that it seemed that Carnes had never made a mistake.

Carnes was a small man with a slight build. He wore his black hair slicked back, had heavy eyebrows, and a pasty complexion from staying on the precinct, avoiding planetfall at every opportunity.

"This way, Captain," said the sergeant, pointing down a dimly lighted corridor.

Carnes moved along, aware that it was humid. The moisture was condensing on the bulkheads, the pipes, and dripping from the overhead. Heat, generated by the engines and power plants, wasn't completely dissipated into space. It radiated upward and outward, to be lost in the lower levels of the precinct.

"Think they use this area," said the sergeant, "because no one comes down here much. Maintenance crews sometimes, but the monitoring stations are all above here."

"How much farther?" asked Carnes, wrinkling his nose at the odor of mildew.

"Around the corner," said the sergeant.

Carnes stopped at the corner. The corridor was brightly lighted with portable lights. A group of men and women stood near them, staring into a hatch. One man was crouched, a video camera held up as he taped everything in front of him.

Carnes walked forward, pushed his way through the crowd, and accidentally kicked the man with the camera.

"Watch it, asshole."

"Your name and rating," said Carnes quietly.

The man took his eye from the camera and looked up. "Sorry, Captain."

"What's going on here?"

"We've got several dead. Murdered."

"How do you know that?"

"Blood everywhere," said the cameraman.

A woman stepped forward. "I'm Sergeant Roberts. First supervisor on the scene."

Carnes turned his attention to her. She was a tall, raven-haired woman with a long, angular face, large eyes, and nearly perfect teeth.

"Tell me," said Carnes.

"We've sealed off the area for what little good it'll do. Got eight people dead by violence. Somebody cut them up . . ."

"What were they doing down here?"

"Drugs. We think that they were all strung out and that's why there is no sign of a struggle."

Carnes peeked around her. The carnage was splattered on the bulkheads and pooled on the deck. The odor of hot copper filled the confined space making Carnes slightly sick to his stomach. He could tell that some of the victims were women.

"Looks like a fairly violent struggle," Carnes observed.

"No, Captain. That's the result of the bloodletting. The victims apparently laid there passively while the killer cut them up. No defensive wounds on the hands, no bruising to show a fight. They were killed as they lay still."

"Drugs?" asked Carnes.

"That would be my guess, but we won't know until we get the autopsy reports."

"You can make a few observations, Sergeant," said Carnes.

"Yes, sir, but they wouldn't be worth much. We just don't have everything we need yet."

Carnes took a step forward, centering himself in the hatch. The sergeant reached out and grabbed his arm to restrain him. "We need to video and photograph this area."

"I'm aware of procedure," said Carnes coldly, but he retreated a step or two.

"We'll be through in a couple of minutes and then we'll be able to enter."

"Right," said Carnes.

The man stood at the back of the crowd, craning his neck so that he could look into the compartment. The bright lights of the investigative team gave the scene a stark reality that had been missing several hours earlier. He watched as others worked around the bodies, filming, taping, and photographing.

"Looks like a slaughterhouse," said a voice beside him.

Without looking, the man nodded. "Worse. How could humans do that to one another?"

"They were as good as dead already. Drug users. Useless. Taking up space and air and food. It's the best thing."

Now the man looked at the speaker, a young woman in a police uniform. She looked as if she had just graduated into the force. Her face was pale, suggesting that her brave words were a cover for a sickness that washed over her.

"You don't look too good."

"You see the tapes. Gruesome tapes of people dead by violence," she said. "Tapes that are tamer than those of the entertainment shows, but when you see it for real, it is different. Those people aren't going to get up again."

"Thought you didn't care."

"I said that they were druggies and they were as good as dead already. That doesn't mean that I approve of the way they died."

"Sure."

She moved forward slightly, got a better look into the compartment, and then retreated. "No one should have to die like that."

The man nodded and didn't speak. Instead he thought that the people deserved to die just like that. They contributed nothing to the precinct. They took and expected more. They felt that the precinct owed them something, owed them food and clothes and support. It didn't matter that they contributed to nothing other than a rising crime rate. They felt that they were owed something and waited for the brass to give it to them.

"Well," said the man, "maybe they have contributed now. A warning to the others."

"The lesson will be lost on the druggies," said the woman. "This is something that happens to others, not to them, if they even know it happened."

"I don't think this is the last time it'll happen," said the man. "There is more here than meets the eye."

• • •

Brackett approached the rear of the crowd and watched for a moment. There seemed to be too many spectators and not enough working cops. People were milling around, just beyond the hatch, watching the fun.

Stopping short, with Daily and Obo right behind him, Brackett put his hands on his hips. Raising his voice slightly, he asked, "Who's in charge here?" When no one responded, he yelled, "Who's in charge here?"

A sergeant pushed her way through the crowd. "I have tactical command for the moment."

"Fine. Get the people out of here who have no business here. There are too many people who can trample the evidence underfoot. We need space to work."

The sergeant didn't move. Instead she hitchhiked a thumb over her shoulder. "Captain Carnes is here."

"He take command?"

"No, Loot. Just here watching the rest of us work."

"Okay," said Brackett. "I'll talk to Carnes but I want everyone out of here unless he or she is involved in searching for evidence or recording the crime scene."

"Yes, sir." The sergeant spun and vanished into the crowd to start the process.

"Obo, why don't you station yourself by that hatch. No one comes in unless he or she has something to contribute to the investigation."

"Sure, Loot."

Daily leaned close and whispered, "What if the criminal has returned to the scene of the crime?"

Brackett stroked his chin and then said, "Have one of the video guys record the crowd before they begin to disperse. I doubt that the man or woman who did this will be in the crowd, but let's do it anyway."

"Okay, Loot."

Carnes appeared suddenly, having shouldered his way through the throng. "Took you long enough to get down here."

Brackett stared at his superior officer but wasn't intimidated by him. Brackett didn't like the little man, believing that he didn't deserve his position, and believing that Carnes didn't like working cops.

"Are you in command here, Captain?" asked Brackett.

"I have not assumed command."

"As senior officer, shouldn't you have done so?"

"I don't need you questioning my decisions. The supervisor here was doing an adequate job and I saw no reason to replace her at the moment. And I don't want you second-guessing me."

"Fine."

"Now that you're here, why don't you take charge. I'll review your performance and if I see anything you've forgotten, I'll let you know."

"Sure."

Carnes turned and was swallowed by the mob. Brackett noticed that Obo was stationed at the rear hatch so that no one would be able to enter. He worked his way through the crowd until he was standing at the hatch and looking at the slaughter in the other compartment.

"Had to be a madman," said a voice near him.

"Rarely," said Brackett. He was thinking of a man, Janos, who was not insane, merely evil. A man who thought of nothing but himself, who killed because it suited him to kill. Insanity didn't enter into it.

He noticed that the people were beginning to filter out of the area, some of them protesting as they went. Obo nodded at them but didn't let any of them turn, and allowed no one to enter who didn't have official business.

The scene in the other compartment did nothing to him. He saw only the bodies of the dead, the splatter patterns on the bulkheads, overheads, and deck. He noticed the positions of the bodies, the drug pipe lying on the deck, and the debris that was scattered around. One woman lay on her back, her shirt ripped open exposing her chest that had been slashed. Those wounds suggested a sexual frenzy, but there was no other evidence of it. Just the dead, killed by something that was sharp.

One of the medical examiners, who had been crouched over one of the bodies, stood and approached him. Peeling the latex gloves from his hands, he said, "All dead. Probably about six hours. Not much more than that. Rigor is just beginning."

Brackett rubbed a hand over his face and then massaged his eyes with the heels of his hands. "Cause of death?"

"I'd say the stab wounds, but I'll want to examine them more closely. One or two of them may have been dead already."

"Meaning?"

"Drugs got them."

"You know the type of drug?"

"Without the toxicology workup, I can't be sure, but the physical evidence suggests a potent form of synthetic opiate."

"Great."

"I'd like to get the bodies up to the morgue as soon as I can."

"Wait one," said Brackett. He stepped through the hatch. The stench of unwashed humans, hot copper, and bowel threatened to overpower him. Breathing through his mouth, he crouched near the closest of the dead. The clothing, where it hadn't been cut, was ragged and dirty. The skin of the hands, where not covered in blood, was filthy. There was grime caked in the hair and grease on the face.

"We have an ID on any of these people?"

"Not yet," said the sergeant who had been in charge. "Computer is looking for a match. We've got the computers working on the fingerprints now."

"Well, I can't believe that all of them were stowaways. We get an ID and it might give us a clue."

Brackett stood up suddenly and turned, walking rapidly from the compartment. There was nothing more that he needed to see. Nothing that wouldn't be visible on the videos or in the holos or in the photographs. Even evidence that was nearly microscopic would appear on the pictures and forensics had a dozen different ways to retrieve it.

Carnes returned and said, "I want this solved in twenty-four hours."

Brackett laughed. "Sure. You should know that it doesn't work like that."

"Lieutenant, I might remind you that I outrank you. But more importantly, the brass here and throughout the system are going to be watching us. This kind of case is a career maker. Or a career breaker. A real ball buster. We need a very quick solution."

Brackett closed his eyes and took a deep breath of the humid air. Not the cool breath of freshness that he wanted to clear his head. Finally, looking at Carnes, he said, "We'll do what we can as fast as we can."

"We just can't allow a mass murder on a precinct," said Carnes.

Brackett nodded and realized that he suddenly had the classic locked-room murder. Someone of the precinct had committed the crime and since they were in deep space, there was no way for the killer or killers to get away. They couldn't escape into space without taking a shuttle and all flights had to be logged in and out. No shuttles were scheduled to leave for the next few weeks anyway. Therefore, the killers had to still be on the precinct. All he had to do was figure out who they were and then go arrest them.

"We're making progress," said Brackett, grinning. "I already have the name of the killer."

"What?"

"It's in the computer somewhere. All I have to do is figure out which one it is."

3 | All the News That's Fit to Print

Wallace Tate, one of the journalists assigned to cover the police beat at the 107th, had heard that something was happening near the engine room. He hadn't bothered to call his editor and hadn't bothered to alert the senior reporter on duty because bonuses were paid to those who uncovered interesting stories. In space it was damned hard to earn a bonus because there was rarely anything of interest happening. It was travel time and dead time until they reached their new patrol zone.

Tate was a tall, skinny kid who had no eyebrows and skin so fair that the hint of a planet's sun burned him if he wasn't careful. He was an awkward kid who managed to stumble over or bump into anything that was out of place, and sometimes over the things that were where they were supposed to be.

Carrying a video camera, an auxiliary recorder, and a notepad, he hurried down toward the engine room, running into those who had been banished from it. At the mid-lift, he stopped a senior sergeant, a man with white hair and a face so full of wrinkles it was impossible to tell much about him.

"What's happening below?" asked Tate.

"Nothing, kid. Everything is fine."

"What were you doing down there?"

"Sightseein'. Hadn't been down there in a long time and I went sightseein'."

"Come on, Sarge, cut me a break," said Tate. He didn't move, blocking the path to the lift.

"Nothing for you to see," said the sergeant. "Nothing going on down there."

"I'll go look for myself," said Tate.

"You do that." The sergeant pushed past him and joined those in the lift.

Tate turned and started down the corridor, suddenly wondering exactly what he was doing there. He'd never ventured into that part of the precinct and, in fact, had heard few stories about it. He'd been told by the old hands that there were areas where the Star Cops refused to go and that those areas had been given over to the "others." Tate had asked about the others, but no one had known much about them. Rumors of people who somehow became lost in the precinct. Maybe they had stowed away, or they had dropped out, or lost their jobs for some reason or another. Cast out of the society, of the precinct, they had drifted lower until they were out of sight.

Tate had never believed the stories, figuring that the old-timers were jerking his chain, just as the veterans had always done with rookies. There were always a hundred good stories that veterans swapped while wide-eyed rookies listened and believed. Up to a point.

Tate had never felt inclined to roam the lower levels because he didn't think there would be any stories there. He stayed near the top, listening as the Star Cops spun their tales, as the brass issued orders, and as the society continued to evolve, everything geared to the solution of crime on planets that couldn't afford real police forces of their own.

Now he was in those lower reaches, in the dimly lighted corridors that suddenly reminded him of the dungeons he'd read about as a kid. The metal bulkheads with no sign of paint or decoration, pipes and wires strung from one end to the other, and the occasional light that did little to chase away the gloom. All it needed were old flaming torches set along the stone walls.

To himself, he said, "All I need is the low moaning of the victims and some dripping water."

He hurried on, stopping at a cross corridor, and then moving beyond it. The stream of people coming up had slowed and then stopped, until Tate was moving along the passageway in silence and alone.

Using metallic steps, and then a system of catwalks, Tate worked his way lower. He reached another corridor. At the end was a blaze of bright light. Tate stopped, used his cameras to record the scene, and then slowly walked forward.

A police officer in uniform, who had relieved Obo ten minutes earlier, stepped out to block his way. "Don't need no sightseeing."

"Press," said Tate.

"Not going to cut it," said the officer. "You turn it on around and head on up and out."

"People have a right to know . . ."

The officer laughed. "Not here they don't. What people you talking about anyway? People here in the precinct? They don't need to know and have no right."

Before Tate could respond, another man walked up. Tate recognized him immediately. "Howdy, Loot. The sergeant here won't let me pass."

"The sergeant is doing his job and when you prepare your story, I hope you'll remember that."

"Sure. You going to let me in to take a look?"

Brackett grinned and said, "I'm not sure that you're going to want to."

"To do a story right, I have to see everything. Otherwise I'm caught without the credibility I need."

"It's okay, Sergeant," said Brackett. "We'll let him in."

"Yes, sir."

"Before we go, I want you to stay back, out of the way. Don't go tramping around where you might destroy evidence. Observe from a distance."

"Can you tell me anything yet?"

"We're still working." Brackett started to turn and then

looked back. "How's this going to set with your friends top-side?"

"When they learn about it, they'll be angry, but by then it will be too late."

"Okay, come with me, but if I tell you to leave or to move, you do it."

"Sure, Loot. Thanks."

They walked across the deck, toward the hatch where another sergeant stood guard. As they approached, Tate tried to see in, but there was a light set at the hatch that made it nearly impossible to view anything beyond it.

"It's not a pretty sight."

Tate ignored the comment and pressed forward until he could see the bodies sprawled on the deck. For a moment, while his eyes adjusted, it looked as if there were bundles of rags on the deck. Then, suddenly, they took on shapes and Tate could see the bodies and the blood.

But he wasn't sickened as he'd thought he would be. Lying in front of him were bodies that had once been human. Now the spark that made them unique was gone and they were nothing more than trash that needed to be collected and disposed of.

Glancing at Brackett, he asked, "What can you tell me?"

"Not much of anything at the moment. We're working on it."

"Right. IDs?"

"Again, we're working on it. I expect to have a press briefing in the morning."

"Sure. Mind if I get some tape?"

"Just be careful," said Brackett.

"Afraid of what it'll show?"

"No. I'm more worried about how people will feel seeing the slaughterhouse as they sit down to breakfast. Use a little discretion. People don't need to see all the blood."

"Right." Tate moved toward the hatch and raised his camera. It was bright enough inside that he didn't need to use his light. He just focused on a police sergeant crouched near a body and taped the man's activities. He swung around slowly, highlighting the work of the police. The blood and the bodies were in the frame as incidental dressing. Props to make the story more real to the viewers.

That's what it had become. The story was no longer important. It was the quality of the visuals that made a story interesting. If the report revolved around something that would affect the life of every living human, it would not get the necessary air play unless there were dramatic visuals to go with it. A murder of drug users in the lower reaches of a ship would get immediate play simply because the visuals were there to support the story.

Finished with the taping, Tate stepped to the rear. "You have a minute to talk to me, Loot?"

"Why don't you catch me later?"

Tate hesitated and then said, "Sure." He turned in time to see Carnes standing near the exit. He hurried over and said, "Get a statement, Captain?"

Carnes blinked rapidly for a moment. He straightened his tie, ran a hand through his hair. "What can I do for you?"

Tate turned on the camera, lifted it to his shoulder, and asked, "What do we have here?"

"Murder," said Carnes dramatically. "A disgusting example of what men can do to one another. And what drugs can do to our society. Even today, with all we know about the effects of various substances on the human body, we have people who abuse themselves."

Tate tried to keep from grinning as Carnes spoke. The captain was trying to sound as if he knew what he was talking about but he wasn't paying attention to the words. The people were abusing themselves. He was sure that Carnes hadn't caught the double meaning of his words.

"As the senior officer on the scene, I have begun the investigation. I was the one who sealed the area and began the search for the perpetrators. I have assumed the command and I guarantee we will find those who committed the crime."

"You said those. That mean there was more than one?"

"I believe that the magnitude of the crime and the numbers involved suggest more than one."

"Do you have a motive?"

"I'm afraid that we don't want to speculate at this time. We'll have to let the investigation lead us to the motivation." Carnes looked suddenly uncomfortable. "If you'll excuse me." Carnes walked out of frame, lifted a hand, and called, "Sergeant, report to me."

Switching the camera off, Tate watched Carnes begin his act. He laughed to himself and said, "Asshole."

An officer Tate didn't recognize appeared at his elbow. "Are you finished?" she asked.

"Getting there . . .?"

"Officer Hastings."

"What do you make of this, Hastings?"

"Nothing. My job is to see that the crime scene isn't contaminated by outsiders. If you are finished, sir, then please vacate."

Tate nodded, thinking that Hastings wasn't that much older than he was. Or maybe she was younger. But she had the authority and he had none. "On my way out."

"Thank you."

Tate stopped outside the area for a moment and glanced back. He saw the turmoil as the police swarmed the corridor and then saw the first of the body bags appear. He hoisted his camera, turned it on, and took what had become a stock shot of multiple death horror. Two people using the handles at the top and bottom of a long black bag, carrying the sagging body from the scene of the crime. He followed their progress as they marched down the corridor until they reached the mid-lift. Dropping the body, they punched the buttons to wait.

Switching off again, Tate hurried forward. When the doors slid open, he waited for the body to be loaded and then asked, "Where are you going?"

"Morgue."

"Yeah."

They rode in silence, the body on the deck. Everyone seemed to be avoiding it. There were no cute jokes, no light-hearted banter. For the first time, Tate realized that he could be in the body bag, and suddenly he was sickened.

4 | Dead Men Do Tell Tales

Brackett stopped outside the morgue and watched through the windows as one of the technicians stripped the body of its tattered clothes and stuffed them into an evidence bag. The bag was labeled and set side. The naked body was photographed, videotaped, and then turned so that every angle could be covered.

Brackett moved to the hatch, waited as it irised open, and then stepped through.

"Howdy, Loot. What can I do for you?"

"I don't suppose you have an ID yet."

"Nope. Just getting started here. Didn't see anything on the clothes to give me a clue. Nothing in the pockets. I'm about to take the fingerprints and cornea prints. Photos will be sent down to ID."

Brackett moved closer and watched as the technician first washed the body, removing the grime and the gore, revealing that it was a white female no more than twenty-five years old. With the body cleaned, the wounds weren't quite as hideous. Slashes in the skin revealed the muscle and in some cases the white bone.

"Nice-looking girl," said Brackett. "Doesn't look like she's been on drugs too long."

"This one doesn't take long."

"You tried the Steelman yet?"

"No. I think this one is too far gone. The probe won't pick up anything useful."

"You don't know until you've tried," said Brackett.

"True enough. You want to use it?"

"Sure."

The technician opened a cabinet and took out the Steelman Probe. It was a small instrument that when placed against the forehead of a recently dead person could, with luck, pick up the last images seen by that person. If the trauma of death wasn't too great, if the brain hadn't been damaged in the death, or if decay hadn't begun, it worked well. After six or seven hours, the images faded to a point where they were useless to investigators.

Setting the Steelman on the autopsy table, he handed the stylus to Brackett. "It's all set."

Brackett took it, pressed it against the dead woman's forehead, and then looked at the digital readout on the face of the Steelman. The numbers were small, indicating that the probe wasn't picking up much.

He shifted it and checked the readout again. Still there wasn't much.

"Could be the drugs. Tends to suppress activity in the brain."

"Don't need much," said Brackett. "Just a picture of the killer. Just a glimpse."

The technician examined the body carefully, starting at the feet and working his way up. "Nothing here except the stab wounds. Looks like she was just beginning to fall into the cycle of malnutrition."

One of the pathologists, Dr. Richard Kimball, entered, holding his hands in the air like a surgeon who was preparing to operate. He nodded at the technician and then said to Brackett, "Good morning, Loot."

"Morning." Brackett glanced at the chronometer set on the bulkhead. It was morning, but just barely. And there was nothing good about it.

Bending over the body, Kimball said, "We've got a young

female dead by violence." He examined the wounds to the chest and then the neck. "Any one of these, or all of them, could be the cause of death. They were inflicted either just prior to or just after death."

"I think," said Brackett, "the toxicology workup will be significant."

"Drug use is evident," said Kimball. He moved to her head, peeled back an eyelid, and studied the eyeball. "Minimal use suggested here. She must have just started."

Brackett watched the readout on the Steelman that wasn't showing much brain activity. He adjusted it again and the numbers faded away. "Lab's going to have a hell of a time with this."

"If she was under the influence of drugs, it's not going to do you any good."

"I'm like the old prospector," said Brackett. "I don't expect to find pay dirt but I always look just in case. We'd be stupid to ignore one of our tools because we don't think it'll work."

"Of course. You about done?"

Brackett shut off the Steelman. "I think that's got it." He pulled the recording cartridge from the Steelman. "I'll take this to the lab. Where are the others?"

"What others?"

"Bodies."

"I think some of them have been taken to autopsy at the hospital so that we can get through this as quickly as possible. Forensics is going to be looking over the case too. And examining the crime scene carefully."

Brackett nodded, knowing that already. He slipped the cartridge into a pocket. "Preliminary results?"

"By noon on this one."

"I'll be looking for it. Carnes is hot for a solution in the next twelve hours."

"Not going to get it," said Kimball.

"I know that, but we've got to dazzle him with the paperwork. He sees us working, even if we're just filling squares, he'll be a happy man."

Kimball moved around the table, touched the dead woman's thigh, and examined the wound there. "The killer used a sharp knife. Very sharp to slice her. Edges of the wound are not ragged, and there is no evidence of threads from her clothes in the wounds."

"Put it all in the report," said Brackett tiredly. "And get it to me."

"Sure thing, Loot."

Brackett walked to the hatch, waited for it to open, and then stepped through. He turned back, looking through the window, and watched as the autopsy began. Normally, he would have watched the whole thing, listening as Kimball dictated his notes to the holo, but this time it wasn't necessary.

He hurried to the mid-lift, entered, and headed to the upper levels. He stopped by his office, turned on the overhead lights, and sat down at his desk. He reached out and touched the computer keyboard but didn't turn on the machine.

"Going to be a long night," said a voice.

Brackett turned and found Daily. "Thought you'd be in your quarters by now."

"I figured I'd better stand by in case there was something that we needed to do."

Brackett reached into his pocket and extracted the cartridge from the Steelman Probe. "You might run this over to the lab and get us a holo of the results. That'll save me some time."

Rather than taking the cartridge, Daily sat down. "How we going to do this?"

"If you mean the investigation, just as we would if we were planetside. One step at a time, following the established procedures, collecting as much data as we can."

Daily shook her head. "That's not exactly what I mean. This case is going to take something more."

"What are you talking about?"

"There an ID on the victims yet?"

"No, but it'll be coming shortly."

Daily took a deep breath and then asked, "Don't you think that is a little strange?"

"Meaning?"

"This is a closed society. Everyone is logged in and out. Computers monitor the assignments of the various people, watch the births in the hospital, the deaths, and every aspect of the whole precinct. There is no one here who has not been registered, regulated, and classified a dozen different ways."

"And now we have eight bodies and no ID."

"Right," said Daily. "I mean, it might take the computers and the technicians a couple of hours to ID them all. Couple of them should have been ID'ed right off."

"Your point?" said Brackett.

"Where in the hell did those people come from? Why can't the computer ID them?"

Brackett was quiet as he thought about it. Finally he said, "Could be nothing more sinister than it's so late and that the night shift doesn't work as hard as the day."

"Could be," said Daily, "but I remember reading a monograph some time ago about stowaways."

"Too many monitors for people to sneak aboard."

"Just something to think about," said Daily.

"Then I have a question for you. Suppose we do have stowaways on board. What do you plan to do about it?"

"I've been thinking about that," said Daily. "I don't have a good idea yet."

Brackett tapped the cartridge from the Steelman. "How about getting that to the lab, then?"

"Sure, Loot." She stood up. "How about catching some breakfast?"

"Little early for that," said Brackett.

"Not now. Later. After I get the results from the lab."

"Okay. I'll give Obo a shout and let him know what we're going to do."

"If you feel you must."

Brackett looked up at her and then remembered what they had been saying to each other when Obo had found them. She had been talking of relationships and working closely together. "Okay," he said. "I won't mention it to Obo."

She picked up the cartridge and said, "See you a little later."

When she reached the lab, she was surprised to find it brightly lighted and filled with people. Then, as she thought about it, she decided it wasn't so surprising. There had been a major crime committed and Carnes had been on the scene. As a good administrator, he would have alerted the head of the crime lab, telling him to get his people in to work.

She walked in and then stopped at the reception area. A young man sat at the desk, reading a computer screen. As she approached, he looked up. "Yeah?"

"Got a Steelman cartridge here."

He hitchhiked a thumb over his shoulder. "See Filkes. In the right lab."

"Thanks."

She entered the lab. It wasn't like most of the crime labs because it was smaller, filled with computer equipment, and had a number of display screens on the bulkheads. There was a single control panel with three chairs set in front of it. A man and a woman manned the panel.

"Got a Steelman," said Daily.

"Give it to me," said the woman. "You're?"

"Daily."

"I'm Walker. That's Filkes. You've got a Steelman from that mass murder?"

"Right."

"Give it here."

Daily handed it over. Walker took it, glanced at the LCD, and then reached out to plug it into one of the slots on the control panel. She touched the keyboard while Filkes worked a number of knobs.

"On the center screen," said Walker.

Daily looked up but there was nothing there except a shadowy, gray mist. It was as if she were trying to see a building through a thick morning fog.

"Contrast sucks," said Walker.

"I'm working on it." Filkes leaned to the left, punched a series of buttons, glanced at the screen, and then straightened. He used two knobs, seeming to twist them in opposite directions.

"This isn't a very good Steelman," said Filkes. "It's at the bottom range."

"Drugs involved too," said Daily.

"Shit." Filkes stood up, walked to another panel, and tried to filter out some of the gray. "I don't know."

Daily pointed. "There."

A shape had appeared on the screen. It was a ghostly image of grays and blacks without much form and no detail at all. It seemed to be crouched, one arm raised.

"Last thing the victim saw," said Walker. "Drugs are screwing us up."

"I don't think it's going to get much better," said Filkes.

But as he spoke, it seemed that the gray ripped for a moment and everything on the screen was clear. The victim was looking past her killer, at someone else moving in the background. The face was in a shadow.

"Can you isolate on that?"

"Retracking now."

Walker grinned. "I'll digitize it and see if we can sharpen the face. On the right screen."

Daily moved forward so that she was directly in front of it. The shape appeared, seemed to focus and then soften. A cursor scanned from the top to the bottom and then up and down. There were black squares scattered randomly over the screen.

"Got the pixels loaded into the computer. Bringing it all up now."

Daily understood the process. The computer was analyzing the data on all sides of the black square and then making a guess as to what would have been in the square had the data been there. Slowly the squares brightened until they were no longer visible.

"Best we're going to get," said Filkes. "I let the computer go, it could sharpen the image, but we begin to lose reliability. Can't say how accurate the picture will be."

"I'll want hard copy of that."

"Certainly."

"Let's run the whole Steelman," said Walker. "We'll get you a holo of it."

Daily retreated to the third chair and watched as the two lab technicians worked. They played with the Steelman for another hour but were unable to clarify the data contained on it.

Filkes finally rocked back in his chair. "That's all we're going to get. Brain was too far gone and the drugs fogged the perceptions."

Walker punched a button and the holo cube popped out. "Here you go."

"You'll make copies from the master?" asked Daily.

"Sure. How many?"

"Half dozen, I suppose. And hard copies of the picture."

"Ship them down to you by noon."

"Good."

Before Daily could leave, Walker asked, "We going to be getting any more Steelmans?"

"I don't know. Lieutenant Brackett did this. I don't think he expected much in the way of results."

"He was right there. We need something a little fresher to work with."

Daily laughed. "I'll tell him you said that, but then, I don't think he was able to do a thing about it."

"Keep telling you people to use the Steelman as soon as

you find the body. Every minute counts. Who knows what we'd have had if the Steelman had been fresher."

"Right," said Daily. She took her holo cube and headed out. They had something, but it wasn't much. But then, no one knew the importance of information when they first got it. Only time would tell.

5 | I'm in Charge Here

Carnes had left the crime scene, gone to his office on the upper levels of the precinct, and then decided that it was time to quit for the day. He watched as the hologram moon over the hologram city set behind the buildings telling him that morning was rapidly approaching.

He'd left, walked to his quarters, and stretched out on his bunk without taking off his clothes or his shoes. He was too tired to think about that. The quiet chiming at the hatch had awakened him a couple of hours later.

Carnes rolled over, put a hand on the deck as if to reassure himself that it was there, and then levered himself up, off his bunk. He staggered to the hatch and opened it.

"Yeah?"

"Captain Carnes, the preliminary reports are back from pathology."

"Give them to me."

The messenger handed over a cube. Carnes took it and plugged it into the terminal. There was a moment of darkness before the screen brightened and the figures and conclusions began to parade across the screen. Carnes pulled the chair out and slipped into it, leaning forward, his chin cupped in his hand.

Stopping the data, he said, "We've gotten no IDs on any of the victims?"

"Not as of about an hour ago."

"They weren't mangled that badly," said Carnes. "Photo ID should have been accomplished."

"All I know is that no one seems to know who they are or where they came from."

"Anyone missing on the precinct?"

"As of now, everyone is accounted for."

"Damn," said Carnes. "Where in the hell did those eight people come from?"

"I don't know. Is there anything else?"

"No. Inform my secretary that I'll be to the office in about an hour."

"Yes, sir."

Carnes turned his attention back to the computer, trying to figure out just what in the hell was going on.

The Cup and Hole was filled with people grabbing their breakfast quickly, but unlike the donut shops of the past, it was possible to get a full breakfast. Brackett, having been up all night, wanted eggs, pancakes, juice, and coffee. He also wanted a shower, about four hours sleep, and a little quiet.

Sitting opposite him, Daily looked as if she had gotten a full night's sleep, though she hadn't. She sat, staring down at a cup of coffee, her donut untouched in front of her.

"Still no ID," she said. "I think it's time that we begin to think in other arenas."

Brackett cut into his omelette, and then said, "What other arenas."

"Time for me to go undercover."

That caught Brackett by surprise. He put down his fork and stared at her. "Undercover? How the hell can you go undercover on the precinct?"

"There are lots of things about this ship that we don't know, or care to know. It's bigger than many old Earth cities, has all the services and facilities, from garbage collection to mall shopping, and it has some of the same problems. There is a whole level, an undercurrent that we never see and therefore ignore."

"Impossible," said Brackett.

"Then how do you explain eight dead bodies that we haven't been able to identify?"

Brackett suddenly found that he was no longer hungry. He pushed his plate away and looked at the holo display along the far bulkhead. It gave a complete view of space around them. Stars set in black velvet. He let his mind drift, thinking about what Daily had said, and then turned his attention back to her.

"What do you have in mind?"

"I've pulled what I could from the computer," she said. "This is one of those topics that people just don't discuss. Out of sight and out of mind. There can't be an undercurrent to life on the precinct. Therefore there is not."

"That doesn't answer the question."

"No, it doesn't. The truth is, I'm just not sure of what I'm going to do. Place to start is down on the retail levels, watching the people there. That's where the dropouts are going to be. No one watching them that closely. No one asking hard questions."

Brackett picked up his coffee and took a sip. "I don't like this."

Daily grinned. "What's not to like? This will be safer than an assignment planetside. I'll be right here on the precinct."

"Undercover work is never that easy," said Brackett. "Infiltrators, informants, and undercover operatives are targets, marked for death because of the danger they present. They're hated because they're stoolies."

"I'll be on the ship. You and Obo will always be close."

"When did you plan to get started?"

"This afternoon, if we don't come up with something on the crime quickly."

Brackett rocked back in his chair and again looked out into space. He'd been on the precinct for more than ten years. He had lived there, worked there, dated and thought of marriage, and then gone back to work. He'd been over most of the levels. Or, rather, most of the upper levels. Rarely had he ventured below the retail level because there was nothing to see there and his work had not taken him there. Suddenly he realized there were large areas of the ship that he'd never seen. Places he'd never gone because he hadn't had to.

"We'll have to work out some way for you to stay in touch with us. Low-level radio maybe."

"Could blow my cover."

"Still, I think that has to be a condition."

"If you insist."

Brackett didn't speak for a moment. Instead he thought of other Star Cops who'd gone undercover. Most of the missions had been successful, simply because those being watched weren't clever enough to figure it out. But there had been some disasters with the bodies of the officers difficult to recognize once they were finally located. Of course, all those other times the undercover work had been done planetside. It wasn't something done on the ship.

"There is the possibility that you'll be recognized."

"I don't think that matters," said Daily. "I don't think they're thinking of undercover."

Brackett finally had a good thought. "I'm going to have to take this to Carnes."

"He won't approve it," said Daily.

"I've got to go to him with this," said Brackett. "It's the only way to run it."

She shrugged. "If you think you must."

Feeling better, Brackett reached out for his breakfast again. He took a bite of the eggs but even cold they tasted good. He had figured out the solution and he wasn't going to be the bad guy.

Brackett found Carnes in his office, the holographic display showing a city that was just beginning the new day. Brackett stood looking at it, wondering how much it cost for the illusion that Carnes was in a skyscraper living on Earth. The illusion was so good that Brackett could have easily been fooled, if he didn't know the truth.

Carnes, sitting behind his massive desk, shuffling papers and tapping sentences into his computer, finally said, "What have you got for me?"

Brackett turned away from the holo and said, "Very little that you don't already know. Steelman didn't provide anything useful. We tried it on all the victims, but they had either been dead too long or their brains were so fogged with drugs that we don't know what the hell we got."

"You should have brought the Steelman down to the crime scene."

"You know that doesn't work well. Too many others standing around. You need a little quiet for it to work. Oh, we did get a single clue. According to the Steelman, there were two killers."

"That's something," said Carnes.

"The problem is that we don't really know what is happening. Sergeant Daily has made a suggestion and I confess that I don't know how good it is. She wants to go undercover."

"Oh, bullshit," said Carnes. He tossed down his pencil in disgust. "I've already heard that she's been trying to get out of the radio duty. Now she comes up with this harebrained scheme. What's with her?"

Brackett remained calm. "She's done the radio watch a couple of times and is familiar with the procedures. She has also made a good point and that is that we haven't gotten an ID on any of the dead."

Carnes looked up with an evil grin on his face. "Shows that you haven't been keeping up with the investigation." He tapped the computer screen. "Got an ID right here."

"What?"

"One of the dead was William David Paulsen, thirty-two."

Brackett moved toward the desk and then stopped, remembering that Carnes outranked him.

"Oh, yes," said Carnes. "Pathologist and the forensic section came up with the name a little while ago and got a match in the computer."

"Who the hell was he?"

"Shop owner. Ran a little boutique that catered to petite women. Came on board about four years ago. Nothing in his file to suggest criminal activity. Computer reports that his shop has been closed for the last five weeks. Bank loan is only one month in arrears, but suppliers have started to complain about late payments."

"Family?" asked Brackett.

"I don't know why you expect me to do your work for you. All this is on the mainframe. I would think that you would check the status of the investigation before you roll in here with stupid plans."

"The plan isn't stupid," said Brackett. "Actually, it would give us a data base for further investigations. There is a real gap in our knowledge about the underground life here."

"That rumor is so much bullshit," said Carnes. "There is no underground. People have been talking about it for twenty years but no one ever offered any proof."

Brackett shrugged because he now believed the rumor. If Carnes thought it was crap, then Brackett knew there had to be something to it. J. Edgar Hoover had claimed that there was no organized crime in America right up until the time the evidence slapped him in the face.

"Then you have no objections to Daily going undercover?"

"It's a waste of manpower but if you feel it will aid in the investigation, then go ahead."

"Certainly, Captain." Brackett stood. "I'll alert her."

"I want daily reports and I'd advise you to watch the investigation a little closer."

"Yes, sir."

It wasn't difficult to find another bunch using drugs. They haunted the lower levels, the dealers and the users, circulating until they found one another and both sides believed they had scored. Then, almost as if they no longer trusted each other, both sides vanished into the corridors, the dealers searching for new customers, and the users searching for a place to take the drugs.

Now, on a catwalk about fifty feet up, the killers watched the buy go down. It was typical. Two people, both women, standing, almost back to back, as if they didn't know each other. The words were whispered and unintelligible on the catwalk, though both men knew what was being said.

There was a flash below as a hand snaked out with a fistful of cash. The drug was dropped to the deck as the dealer walked away hurriedly. The watchers let the dealer go. She wasn't of interest to them.

The user stooped and snatched the cellophane envelope from the deck. She held it at eye level, studying the contents for a moment, and then stood up. Looking right and left, up and down the corridor, she walked rapidly toward the lower reaches of the ship.

"Let's go," said the bigger of the men.

"I'm right behind you."

Staying on the catwalk, they could shadow the woman. She wasn't looking up. Just staring at the deck in front of her as she worked her way lower.

They came to a ladder and scampered down it and then ran forward so that they could watch the woman. She reached a hatch, hesitated, and then entered without even looking back to see if she had been followed.

"That'll be it."

"What's in there?"

"Storage of some kind."

They reached the hatch, took positions on either side of it, but didn't move again. The bigger man put an ear against the bulkhead but heard nothing from inside the cabin. The engines hidden so far below them rumbled, sending vibrations through the lower regions. He detected that, not sure if he heard them or felt them.

"They should be out of it by now."

The man pulled his knife. He studied the blade, gleaming in the half-light of the corridor. It was a fine instrument, crafted carefully by an artist. He then centered himself in front of the hatch and watched as it irised open.

The woman who'd bought the drug lay sprawled on the deck, faceup. Both her arms were raised as if she were a small child asking a parent to pick her up. Her unseeing eyes were fixed on a point on the bulkhead near the overhead.

Two others were there. One was slumped against a bulkhead and the other lay flat on the deck. None of them seemed to have the slightest clue about what was happening around them. They were unconscious.

"I'll kill the woman," said the bigger man as he crouched next to her.

"Sure."

He entered and knelt beside her. He looked down at her, surprised because her face wasn't as dirty as those of most users. She wore makeup, eye shadow, and her clothes were clean, looking as if they'd been pulled from the closet only that morning. Her hair wasn't the normal tangled mess and there was no dirt caked under her fingernails. She hadn't been living the life very long.

"Too bad," said the man. "You should have stayed home." He pressed the tip of his knife against her stomach and slowly increased the pressure until it cut through the clothing and rested on her skin.

"What?" she asked, starting to sit up.

"Nothing." He pushed harder and felt the blade slip easily into her body. He felt the blood begin to flow, warm against his hand. She fell back, groaned low in her throat, but didn't move again.

Pulling the knife from her, he stood up and looked down as she died. It was a slow process, her blood soaking into her clothes and then beginning to pool slowly under her. Her face became pale and then waxy, looking unreal and lifeless. Staring into her eyes, he saw them cloud over as the spark of life fled suddenly.

"I'm ready."

His partner stood and grinned broadly at him. His weapon

was held loosely in his left hand, the blood dripping from it to splatter the deck. "They're dead too. Won't be using drugs again."

"Yeah."

Together they left the supply room. Neither looked back. In the corridor, they saw no one. They had gotten away with it again.

6 | The Price Is Right

Brackett, having a few spare moments, called up the report that he was supposed to be writing, and wondered where Daily had disappeared to. She had promised she would help, but that was before the nonsense of going undercover had come up. Still, she should have reported in, simply because she didn't know if she'd gotten approval.

The cursor blinked quietly at him, telling him that there was work to do, but he still couldn't get started. The events of the night before intruded, and the words of Captain Carnes rang in his ears. The screen remained blank.

Tate appeared, tapped on the bulkhead, and asked, "You busy, Loot?"

"Always busy, but getting nowhere," said Brackett. He turned so that he could look at the reporter, deciding that any diversion was better than staring at the screen. He called it work avoidance.

"Anything new?"

Brackett stroked his chin. "Now there's an interesting question. Just what are you looking for?"

Encouraged by Brackett's attitude, Tate took a step forward. "Anything new on the crime last night?"

"Nothing that is going to appear on the videos tonight, if that's what you mean. We're working."

"That's what you cops always say. Just like the doctors who say, 'He's doing as well as can be expected.' "

"Well, the last thing we want to do is tell the bad guy what we know. That drives him underground. Makes our job that much harder. If you wanted to help, you'd interview the bad guys, spreading their plans all over the video." Brackett nodded solemnly. "Yeah. I think the next time some smart-ass reporter is demanding that I do something, I think I'll suggest that he get the rest of the story from the bad guy."

"Which all means that you don't know squat."

"Which means," said Brackett, "that there are things happening, but nothing that we can let you have."

"Yeah."

Brackett started to turn back to his computer report and then stopped. "Say, Wally, you get down on the commercial level much?"

"Sure. Lots to do down there."

"Why don't you and I head down there then. Look around and see how the other half lives."

"If you're working on something, I have the right to know," said Tate.

"No, you don't. You have the right to get out of here. You have the right to stay off this level. You have the right to never get another story out of any of us. Or, you could be a good boy and just walk around with me. Then, if something breaks, you'll be right there."

"I'll need to check with my editor."

"No, you don't. You're stalling for time." Brackett stood. "You can go down with me or you can just forget it."

"Sure, Loot. What are you looking for?"

Brackett ran a hand through his hair as he thought about it. "That's the question of the hour. I don't know. I just don't get down there much. Support crews, families, lots of people go down there, but I never have much need of it."

"Everything that you could want is available down there," said Tate.

"Everything?"

Tate hesitated and then nodded. "If you know the questions to ask, where to ask them, and spread a little money around, you can get anything."

"Women?"

"If you want. Or men if that's the way you think. Kinks? Sure. Everything you can think of. Some of them cost a lot and some of them cost almost nothing."

"I don't know why I'm surprised," said Brackett. "That's the way it's always been. Followers and hangers-on who trail behind the armies and the camps. There will always be things that must be done and people willing to do them."

"Don't let me give you the wrong impression," said Tate. "It's not quite like that."

Brackett turned off the computer and the lights and waved at the corridor. "Lead the way."

"Anything that comes up, I have exclusive. You let me report it first."

"As long as it doesn't hurt the investigation."

They took the mid-lift down, let the doors open, and then stood for a moment, looking out. The corridor was wider than those above and the overhead was twenty feet from the deck. Rather than hatches, there were windows and open doors. Neon flashed in a few of them.

The thing that Brackett noticed was the crowd. They were shoulder to shoulder, circulating in the area between the storefronts. Thousands of people moving with the same slow cadence, looking like the currents of a gently flowing river. Up one side and down the next. There were a few benches, like boulders in the water. The crowds parted as they flooded around the benches.

"Now I remember why I never come down here. Too many people."

Tate exited, waited for Brackett, and then joined the crowd. A quiet murmur washed over them. Somewhere a kid screamed his displeasure and a second cried continuously.

"This is all some people have to do," said Tate. "Their jobs have been eliminated by automation, or they've been fired, or they've just run out of steam and quit."

Directly in front of them were two men who looked as if they hadn't changed clothes in a month. Their hair was long and dirty. They smelled as if they had never bathed.

One of them broke from the crowd and slipped toward the open door of a deli. He was met by the proprietor who handed him a grease-smeared sack. Grinning, the man slipped back into the crowd and held the bag up like it was a trophy.

"That shows you how some of them stay alive."

Brackett nodded his understanding. The owner of the deli didn't want the dirty man inside. Rather than argue with him, he provided a little food. Everyone got what he wanted. The owner kept the vagrant out and the dirty man got a little free food. No problem.

They walked along, drifting with the crowds. Brackett glanced into windows that showed a variety of products from those to eat, to those to wear, to those to view. There were small restaurants, boutiques, video stores, and arcades. Each of them seemed to be packed, some with children wasting an afternoon, others with adults trying to buy the necessities of life, and still others with people eating.

The noise level on the mall was low. Metal bulkheads had been covered with sound-absorbing cloth. The metal deck was carpeted, and the overhead, above the lights, was tilted and baffled so the sound wouldn't bounce back.

"Quiet," said Brackett.

Tate didn't respond as they walked along. To the left, set in the center, were more of the benches. Some of them were occupied by people resting for the moment. Others had been staked out, as if they were being homesteaded by people in ragged clothes. They lay there, as if daring someone to try to sit.

They reached the end of the level where there were elevators and escalators that would take them back up to the working levels or down into the living levels of the support crews. There were other narrower corridors that led into working areas of the ship. Sitting at the entrance to one was a woman in a dirty coverall who looked as if she hadn't moved in a month.

Turning, to head up the other side, Tate said, "This is where they come. No one patrolling this area. They can get handouts and find a warm, safe place to rest."

"How did it happen? How did these people get on the precinct?"

Tate shrugged. "We haven't done much with it. We've interviewed a few on the video, but only to expose their plight. Here they are, in a closed society where everyone supposedly has a job, enough to eat, and a cabin to use. But we find some living on this level or below in a hand-to-mouth existence. We tell that side of the story but we don't ask them how they got here. What happened to them."

"Why not?"

"I don't know. Maybe because the sight of a couple of kids with dirty faces and the need for a place to stay and food is easy to deal with. People contribute to get them off this level and back into school and then feel they have accomplished something important."

"Which they have," said Brackett.

"True enough. But if we start to explore the reasons for it, people don't get the warm fuzzy feeling. Someone had to do something rotten to create the situation and people might not be able to correct it, so we ignore the cause and attack the symptom. Eliminate the symptom and everyone is happy."

Brackett stopped abruptly and a man walked into him. "Hey, asshole. Be careful."

"Yeah," said Brackett idly. He was looking at the two people sitting on the bench. Neither of them looked as if they belonged on the precinct. They were short, dirty, and ragged. They huddled together as if drawing strength from each other.

Brackett moved toward them, waited until one of them looked up, and said, "What's your name?"

"Who wants to know?"

"Brackett."

"Well, Brackett, why don't you just fuck off and leave us the hell alone?"

Tate tugged at Brackett's arm. "They're not going to talk to you."

Brackett held his ground, staring down at the man and woman. He locked eyes with the man until he looked away nervously.

"Let's go," said Tate.

Brackett hesitated, knowing that he could get the information if he wanted it. He had the authority to challenge anyone on the precinct. He could drag them to the holding cells and then interrogate them until he knew everything there was to know. He could hold them indefinitely if they had no pass for the precinct and had no sponsor. That would mean they were criminals because they would have boarded illegally. Knowing all that, he was surprised at the belligerence.

Again Tate said, "Let's go."

"Yeah, man. You'd better go."

For just an instant, Brackett felt an anger burn through him. He was going to drag them to the holding area on general principles. And then he knew that there was no reason. If he didn't get the answers from them, then he could find someone else. Too many people seemed to be dropouts.

He joined Tate. "You'd think they'd want to maintain a low profile."

"Nothing makes sense here," said Tate. "Have you seen enough?"

"Nope," said Brackett. "I don't understand this." He waved a hand at the mall.

"Where else can they go?"

"No, that's not what I mean. Why do there seem to be so many? Why have they dropped out?"

"Maybe because they see no point in wasting their lives struggling to make ends meet while the brass suck the life blood from them. If they do away with their material possessions, then they have no reason to continue to work. They know that they won't starve. Somehow they'll get fed. Shelter is no problem. Hell, this is an enclosed environment. So I guess they ask themselves why work when they can do nothing at all and have their freedom."

"You know that for a fact or are you making it up?"

Tate had to grin. "I think I've given you what I think is the ideal answer. The people who dropped out did it from some kind of noble inspiration. Probably they're just too lazy to work. Or the system has conspired against them."

"So you don't know either."

"You'd need a sociological study to find the truth. Someone with the proper training would have to spend some time looking into all the reasons . . ."

"Someone like Daily?"

"If she remembers anything from school. How long has she been a cop?"

"Long enough to make sergeant."

"Which tells me nothing."

Brackett stopped again and saw Obo towering over the crowd. The Tau was searching the faces as he passed them, working his way against the flow.

Brackett lifted a hand and Obo spotted him. The Tau forced his way closer and then stopped. "There has been another one."

"Another what?" asked Brackett.

Obo looked at the reporter, and the other people still moving around the three individuals who had stopped. He waited until the people started moving again. "Another murder," he said, his voice low.

"Where?"

"Below. Just three people."

Brackett turned and looked back over his shoulder. Nothing had changed on the ship. "You got the details?"

"Nothing more," said Obo. He stood his massive hands on his hips, towering over everyone around him.

"Let's go on down."

Tate grabbed at Brackett. "I'm going with you." It wasn't a request.

"Sure," said Brackett. "But you're not authorized to release anything without approval."

"Nope."

"Then you're not going," said Brackett. "Obo?"

"He won't go."

Tate knew his bluff had been called. "Nothing until you authorize it."

"Fine."

7 | What Goes Around Comes Around

Carnes, who had been enjoying his morning because he'd had the privilege of chewing out a number of his subordinates, now was in a bad mood. It started when his secretary, a robot that was built to be attractive and to fill the role of a secretary, opened the door and stuck her head in. She merely announced that he was wanted in the inspector's office at his earliest convenience. Naturally there was nothing in her voice to convey excitement.

Carnes, who had crawled up the chain of command not because he was a superior police officer or a first-rate investigator but because he understood the politics of the system, knew that the inspector meant immediately. He looked at the papers scattered on his desk, at the computer screen filled with numbers, and then thought of all the work he had to do. Talking to the inspector, if it went as it normally did, would eat up an hour of valuable time.

"Please tell the inspector that I'll be there in five minutes," said Carnes.

"Certainly," said the secretary, bobbing her head. She disappeared a moment later.

Standing, he punched a couple of computer keys, to save the material in the memory, and then shut down the system. He walked to the hatch, made sure that everything was where he wanted it, and then headed out. To his secretary, he said, "I'll be in the inspector's office and then I'll be coming right back here."

"Yes, sir," she said, smiling.

Carnes was almost to the inspector's office when the inspector appeared. Jason Dunlop had made his way up the chain in the same fashion as Carnes. Neither was an investigator. Both were administrators.

"Come on," said Dunlop. "There's been another killing."

"What?"

"Below. Three people. I want you to get down there and take charge. I'll be with you to oversee."

Carnes nodded but wanted to refuse. He was being sandbagged the same way that he had sandbagged Brackett. Dunlop would take credit for any success but burn Carnes if the investigation failed.

"I've assigned Lieutenant Brackett to the case," said Carnes.

"This is becoming a hot issue," said Dunlop. "Besides, since your sister died . . ."

"That is unrelated to this. She was in the hospital. She had a reaction to the anesthetic."

"Drugs are drugs," said Dunlop. "Now, are you going to keep whining or are you going to obey your orders."

"Orders," said Carnes, his voice low so that it was almost impossible to hear him.

They spun and hurried down the corridor to the mid-lift. As they stood waiting, Dunlop said, "Don't have much information. Maintenance crews found the bodies about twelve minutes ago. Area's been sealed but the killer is long gone."

The lift arrived and the doors opened. Dunlop stepped in and hit the button to take them lower.

Carnes asked, "Someone got a Steelman?"

Dunlop shook his head. "Doubt it will do any good. Sounds like the people have been dead for a while."

"Shouldn't we take one down with us just in case?"

"When we get there we'll have the uniforms alert the medical crew. They can bring one."

"Yes, sir."

The doors opened on a long, brightly lighted corridor. There was a cluster of people at the far end, all standing around, trying to see something beyond them. Carnes and Dunlop reached them, pushed their way beyond them, and finally found themselves standing in front of the open hatch. Three people were in the cabin, crouched over the bodies of the dead.

Entering, Dunlop demanded, "What have we got here?"

One of the three stood. She was a young woman in uniform. "We've got three people dead by violence. Stabbed. No ID on any of them at this time."

"You are?"

"Sergeant Sheila Koelher."

"How long have they been dead?"

"Maybe eight hours. Maybe less. Cabin is so warm that it's accelerated the decomposition making estimates difficult."

"Where is the medical examiner?"

"On the way down."

Dunlop looked at the bodies. To Carnes, he said, "I want you to take over now."

"Yes, sir."

Carnes moved forward and crouched near the head of the dead woman. Her face was calm, looking as if she had no idea that she was being murdered. Carnes reached for her hand and looked at it. No defensive wounds. She hadn't tried to save her life. She just let the killer cut her up.

"What about the men?" he asked.

Koelher pointed at them. "About the same. Dead as long, no ID and no sign of a struggle."

Carnes stood and backed away. He glanced at Dunlop, wondering what the inspector wanted done next. The Steelman hadn't arrived, but since the estimated time of death was so long ago, he doubted the Steelman would be of any use.

"Let's get this place sealed off," said Dunlop, more to hear himself give an order than because too many people were entering.

Carnes, near the door, asked again, "Where's the medical examiner."

"On the way."

Brackett, as they hurried down, had the feeling that the news was going to be bad. The untimely death of strangers was one thing, especially those who lived on another planet, but the people were being killed on the precinct. They could be friends. And the thought that kept spinning around his head was that he hadn't seen Daily since she had decided to go undercover. He didn't think that she had begun the assignment, but he didn't know for sure.

They stopped at the end of the corridor and looked at the gapers. The criminal often returned to the scene of the crime and Brackett was studying the faces, looking for someone he recognized who shouldn't be there.

"Obo, I want video of everyone in this mob."

"Of course, Loot."

They pushed through the crowd, stopped at the hatch, and surveyed the cabin. Brackett didn't like the number of people on the scene. Too many feet to tramp through the area, covering up the little evidence and destroying the few clues. The problem was that most of the people in the cabin were senior police officers down there because it was close and they could feel like real cops again.

Carnes noticed Brackett, lifted a hand, and said, "Lieutenant. Glad that you could get here." He moved forward.

Brackett had hoped to avoid the brass but now there was no way to escape.

Carnes said, "I've ordered a Steelman."

"Probably no good," said Brackett. "Too long and the

mind fogged with drugs. Got nothing much from the last ones."

"Still . . ."

Brackett ignored that. He made sure that Obo was getting pictures of everyone standing around. Tate was being held back with the spectators.

The crime scene, Brackett saw, mirrored the last one, except the number of dead was fewer. He spotted Koelher and walked over to her for a quick briefing. Koelher filled him in, just as she had Carnes, and then got the hell out of the way. Koelher knew that heads would roll if the crime wasn't solved quickly and the best way to keep her head on her shoulders was to stay away from the brass.

Brackett saw no sign of a weapon, saw nothing that would provide him with any kind of clue. Enough people had already been inside the cabin that there was a better than even chance that the scene had been compromised.

He realized that what he needed was an idea of where the killer, or killers as the last Steelman had suggested, went after the crime. They should have been splattered with blood. Arteries pumped blood in sprays and it looked as if more than one artery had been severed. The killers must have had blood on them as they escaped.

He remembered reading a book about Lizzie Borden where the author suggested that she had committed the crimes in the nude, washing the blood from her body and hair before anyone saw her. That way there were no blood-stained clothes to convict her.

Of course, two or more killers walking the corridors in the nude would call attention to themselves. While nudity was accepted on the precinct, given the living arrangements, it wasn't that common.

"Closest crew shower areas?" asked Brackett.

Koelher shook her head.

"Find out." Turning, he called, "Obo, get these people out of here now. Nothing to see."

"Yes, Loot."

He stood back and took in the scene. It was no different than the other. He could feel a chill, as if the killers were still there. It was a cold-blooded crime. With no defense wounds on the hands of either victim, it meant they put up no resistance. It took a cold person to be able to slaughter other humans that way.

"What are you going to do?" asked Carnes.

"I think we're going to have to seal off these areas. Patrol them as if we were a force in a city on Earth. Crimes are being committed here so we flood the area with cops. Surveillance cameras up all over."

"Should have done that after the first murders."

"At that time we didn't know there would be more crimes. Now we have that information."

Kimball appeared in the hatch, carrying a black bag like a doctor of the past. He stood for a moment and asked, "Someone call for a doctor?"

"What can you tell me?" asked Brackett.

Carnes interrupted. "Did you bring the Steelman?"

"I've got it, but I think there are too many people around here for it to be effective."

"Let's get it working."

Kimball looked at Brackett who nodded his approval. Kimball took the stylus out, checked the power, and then placed it between the eyes of the female victim. "Who did this?" he asked her, hoping to focus the psychic energy.

Brackett knelt next to the readout, watching the numbers on it. "You're getting nothing."

Kimball shifted the probe and kept up the stream of questions. He leaned down and yelled into her ear, hoping that something would penetrate the dead brain.

"Nothing," said Brackett. "No readings."

"Let's try the man," said Carnes.

Kimball shot him a look of anger but then switched without a word. The process began again.

And again it failed. Nothing registered at all. Kimball tried a dozen different places on the male victim's head, but finally gave up. "Don't know why I expect anything. Only works about one time out of a hundred."

"It's good procedure," said Carnes.

Brackett grinned at that. Good procedure didn't always translate into good detective work. There were times that procedure protected the investigator but there were times when procedure got in the way of hunches. Sometimes there were things a good detective saw, at a subliminal level that directed him away from procedure. Unfortunately, this wasn't one of those times.

Kimball said, "Steelman isn't working."

"Then secure it," snapped Carnes.

An officer arrived and stood at the perimeter of the little group, watching. Brackett focused his attention on the man and said, "What is it?"

"Found a crew shower at the end of the corridor that has been used recently."

"The killers?" asked Brackett.

"Don't know, Loot. We pulled the drain and found a little bit of blood but it was so diluted that we couldn't tell much about it. They might be able to type it . . ."

"What do you think, Doc?" asked Brackett.

Kimball shrugged. "Could have been a crewman who cut himself. Blood type won't do you much good. Odds are that the type will match one of these victims, but that'll prove nothing."

"You secured the area?"

"Certainly, Loot. And we're going over it carefully now, just in case."

"Keep me informed if you find anything useful."

"Sure." The man, having finished his report, spun and hurried off.

Now Brackett turned back to Kimball. "Well, Doc?"

"Three people dead by violence. I'll know more after the autopsy." He packed the Steelman and then stood. "Anything else you want?"

"They are dead," said Brackett.

"As a doornail," said Kimball. "Whatever that is. Obvious that they're dead."

"Had to ask the question," said Brackett.

"Right."

Carnes moved closer and asked, "Isn't there something else that you need to do?"

"Like what? The area has been searched. Everything has been photographed by every kind of camera. The medical examiner has pronounced the victims dead. We found a shower area that the killer or killers might have used and that is being searched, though I doubt we'll get anything from it. We need to get the victims out of here and begin the field interviews, including everyone who showed up down here."

"Then get with it," said Carnes. He slipped away, toward the inspector.

Brackett looked at Kimball and laughed. "The brass have no idea of what they're doing."

"That's why they're the brass."

"Exactly."

8 | Sometimes You Just Have to Fade into the Background

Daily had been so sure that her plan would be approved, especially since there didn't seem to be any other leads, that she had headed back to her cabin. It was a single room on the deck just above the Cup and Hole with no shower facility. That was shared with three other female personnel, not all of whom were assigned as Star Cops.

The bunk folded down out of the bulkhead so that when she wasn't sleeping, it was out of the way. There was a tiny desk with a computer keyboard and display screen that could be used to receive the regular broadcast channels. The whole cabin was not much more than six by six, but it was hers alone and that made it special. It was also one of the benefits of being a Star Cop. Some of the others—the merchants, suppliers, and support people—had to pay monthly rent.

She had stripped her uniform, hanging it out of the way, and then searched through the drawers, also built into the bulkhead, trying to find the kind of clothes that she thought someone who had lost her job, who was without a place to live, would wear. The problem was that everything looked too new and too good for her assignment.

"Well, after a couple of days, that'll change," she said to herself.

She put on jeans, a light shirt, and then a jacket. She ripped at the sleeve of the jacket, tearing it slightly. She also tore out the knees of her jeans, making them look a little more ragged.

Finished, she closed up everything, made sure that the power was off to her computer since she wouldn't be using it for a couple of weeks, and took a final look around the cabin. It was small, but it was comfortable. It was a lot more comfortable than the areas in the lower regions of the ship. She was sure that she would miss it before too long.

She left, headed up toward Brackett's office to make sure that she had approval, but when she got there, Brackett was gone. She left him a note to tell him that she had gone undercover, never thinking that the last thing a woman going undercover should do is announce the fact in writing and then leave it unguarded for prying eyes. She saw it as letting her superior know that she was on the job.

Now she headed down to the commercial level, taking the mid-lift most of the way, and then using the escalator. She joined the crowds, walking with them, watching them as a few began the ritual of begging for food or new clothes or shelter for the evening.

She drifted into a couple of shops, but since her clothes were clean, no one intercepted her at the door. She watched as a young woman was chased from a deli, and then left after her, following her.

The woman entered a dozen other shops, coming out of one with a donut and another with part of a sandwich. She worked her way to a bench and sat down to devour the sandwich like a lion after a kill. She concentrated on the task, glancing up occasionally, as if she expected the jackals to appear, trying to steal her food.

A man, dressed no better than she was, dropped out of the crowd, stood off watching her eat, and then slowly moved in. He sat at the far end of the bench stealing glances at her as she finished the sandwich. Slowly he moved toward her.

Daily decided that these were people she wanted to know. She slipped closer but didn't sit on the bench. Instead she watched the ritual as the man tried to talk the woman out of part of the donut. The woman broke a chunk off part of it and handed it to the man.

That surprised Daily. Here was a woman down on her luck, living hand to mouth, and yet she was sharing the little she had with a stranger.

They finished eating and stood up. Together they joined the crowd. Daily followed them as they worked their way along the mall, heading toward the exit at the far end. They disappeared through the hatch, taking one of the lifts down, toward the lower levels.

Daily missed the lift, but got the next one. She rode down four or five levels and exited. Now she was in a nearly deserted corridor. She walked along, searching the cabins and rooms off it. There were a few people scattered around. Some of them sleeping, some of them sitting in stupors, but none of them seemed very active.

Daily finally entered one of the cabins and took a vacant spot on the deck.

"Can't stay there," said a voice.

"Why not?"

"That's Bill's. Comes in about two, three hours from now. Always got a bottle."

"He'll just have to find a different place," said Daily.

"Don't work like that. You don't take another's space. Ain't done."

Daily turned her attention to the speaker. He was a short man who looked to be about fifty. His hair was salt and pepper and his beard was sprinkled with white. Deep wrinkles etched his face, defining his eyes that were dark brown.

"Where can I go?"

"You're new, ain't ya?"

"What do you mean?"

Bill laughed and slipped closer to her. She could tell that he hadn't bathed in a number of days. The filth was ground into his clothes.

"I mean that you don't know the ropes. Looks like you've been eatin' good lately."

"What happened to you?" asked Daily.

Bill shrugged. "Nothin' much. Just got tired of the grind. Tired of having to hit the store at five and stayin' there until six or seven. Never enough . . ."

The man fell silent and looked at her carefully. "What's it to you?"

"Nothing," she said.

"You got anything to eat?"

She shrugged.

"Should've brought something. Shouldn't show up with nothing in your pocket."

Daily was becoming uncomfortable. Bill had slipped into her personal space. His breath was terrible. He leered at her as if he saw her as something he could use in some fashion. The look duplicated that of the woman who had gotten the sandwich.

Standing, she asked, "Where can I sit?"

Bill patted the deck next to him. "Right here, darlin', I'll take care of you."

"Don't need anyone to take care of me," she said.

"Maybe not right now, but you will."

Daily slid toward the hatch. She stepped out into the corridor. There was pecking order, or a societal structure, even with those who had dropped out. Not that it surprised her. She knew that the human being was a social animal, and except for a few individuals who were happier by themselves, they formed groups. Any group had a leader, even if that leader did nothing more than determine who got the best resting place. Obviously she was going to have to move carefully.

She walked down the corridor, passed two people lying on the deck just inside a shadow that hid them slightly. They were lying face-to-face and Daily couldn't tell if they were men or women or one of each.

She reached the end of the corridor and either had to turn back or go lower. She walked down the escalator that was broken. At the bottom, she noticed more people. They lined the bulkheads, sitting, lying, or standing. They weren't talking to one another. There was very little communication.

Each of the people had their possessions close to them. A bag stuffed with more clothes, or a box holding extra shoes or maybe a bottle or two. They guarded those like the owner of a bank guarded the vault.

No one seemed to care that she had moved into the area. They didn't look up at her and didn't speak to her. It was as if she didn't exist.

There was an empty space and she dropped into it. She made sure that she was touching nothing that belonged to anyone else. She worked at avoiding eye contact with any of the others. Time was going to move slowly, but that was how undercover work went. Spend days, weeks, or even months, setting up the role so that the information would finally begin to flow.

The problem was that she didn't have weeks. Maybe a couple of days and probably only a few hours.

Obo had followed his instructions, had then followed Brackett back to the upper levels, and finally had been sent off on his own. The 107th Precinct was a huge place, filled with all kinds of people. Though the majority of them were human, many of whom had actually been born on Earth, a sizable minority were alien, born on planets scattered through the known portion of the galaxy, and who had no ancestry that could be remotely classed as human.

Some of them looked human. There were people who could pass, unless someone took a close look at them. There were those with reptilian features and no hair. Some were taller than humans, others shorter, and still others whose skin was blue or green or flaming orange. It was a cross section of the galaxy, assigned to the precinct so that there would be someone, or something, who could understand the subtleties of the various races and cultures. It was the clues found in those subtleties that sometimes broke a case wide open.

Obo, being from Tau Ceti, was not human. He was much

taller, much stronger, and covered with a peachlike fuzz that made his body appear green in normal sunlight. In the artificial lights of the precinct, the slight irregularities of his fuzz were visible, and the color sometimes shifted toward the red. Making fun of his red fuzz was the quickest way to make him mad.

Since his arrival and assignment to Brackett's team, he had learned English. At first he was barely understandable, but lately he had acquired an English accent. It amazed people to hear the "King's" English coming from a creature raised on a planet more than thirteen light-years from Earth and Great Britain.

Now he had his assignment and had left the administration levels of the precinct. He was wandering the commercial level that catered to those not of human origins. It did not have the neatness or the organization of the mall that was patronized by the humans.

Obo was now attired as a native of his home world and not as a member of the Star Cops. He wore a vest that left most of his chest bare, pants that came only to his knees, and then soft leather boots that covered his lower leg and most of his calf. He wore a knife at his hip, but on the precinct it was more ceremonial than functional.

The commercial level for aliens was not a straight shot as it was for the humans. It was a meandering lane with shopfronts that seemed to reach out. The interiors of some looked as if they had been lifted from the planets where the owners lived. There were electronic screens that allowed the customers to pass through, but held the environments intact. Some were dark and damp, others bright and wet, and a few hot and dry. For those searching, they could find a shop, store, or center that contained a fair representation of the environment on their home world.

Obo stopped in front of a store that was brightly lit on the inside. The light was an orangish color and the interior was hot. Obo pushed his way in and stood in the soft, fine sand like that from his home world. He wanted to take off his boots and wiggle his toes in the soil but resisted the temptation.

At the far end was a small bar with another giant standing behind it. When he saw Obo, he lifted a hand. In the native tongue, he called, "Welcome, son."

Obo hurried across the sand and stopped short, lifting his hand in response. "Thank you for your hospitality. A breath of home."

"I have anything that you might want. Everything that you could find at home."

"Trogdone?"

"Of course. In both flavors. Hot and cold."

"A tankard. Cold."

The Tau turned, bent, and filled a tankard. He placed it on the bar directly in front of Obo. He waved off a payment. "First one is on the house. Once you learn where we are, I figure you'll be back for more."

Obo sipped the trogdone and set the tankard on the bar. "Get many newbies in here?"

"Some. Especially those from home."

"Anyone recently?"

"Not in the last week or so. Couple came in. Just arrived at the precinct and were surprised that I was here. Nice couple. He's got something to do with maintenance."

Obo reached out for the tankard. He lifted it but didn't drink. "Anybody in here who doesn't really fit?"

"What the hell does that mean? You a cop or something?"

"Just looking for an old friend. He's a little on the weird side. That's all." He sipped the drink.

The owner slipped to the rear and picked up a tankard. Using a towel, he began to polish it carefully.

Obo finished his trogdone. He smacked his lips loudly, as was the custom at home, and slammed the tankard to the bar. "Best I've ever had."

The owner grinned broadly. "Tell your friends."

"Of course." Obo exited and then stood looking at the other aliens. He was no longer sure how to proceed.

9 | That Was No Laser, That Was My Knife

Brackett decided that he wasn't going to wait for the report to come down from Kimball. He was going up to hear it before it was written out. Sometimes things got lost in the translation from mouth to page to eye.

Kimball was sitting in a cabin off to one side of the autopsy room. Brackett walked through the brightly lighted area, past the autopsy table that was again sparkling clean, and across the empty deck. He reached Kimball's office, tapped on the bulkhead, and waited until Kimball waved him in.

Dropping into one of the visitor chairs that was bolted to the deck, Brackett said, "What can you tell me?"

"Victims were under the influence of drugs, though the woman hadn't been a user long. Maybe just a week or so. Certainly no more than two weeks."

"You get an ID on her?"

"Info is down at records and they're scanning now. I would imagine that we'll get a hit on her. Haven't been to port or had a major influx of people in the last week, which means she had to come from the inside population."

"What about the men?" asked Brackett.

"Longtime users. Six months at least. And had either survived, he would have been dead in another six months." Kimball blinked suddenly, as if he just understood what he'd said. "I mean that if they continued to use at the rate they had been, it would have killed them anyway."

"What the hell are they using?"

Kimball rocked back in this chair, laced his fingers behind his head, and stared at the overhead. "It's a synthetic drug, easy to manufacture and instantly addictive. Most drugs, there is a period where you can stop fairly easily. Not with this. One hit and you're hooked. Psychological and physical. Doesn't give you a chance to quit."

"This is something new?" said Brackett.

"On the precinct? Yeah, fairly new. Saw the first indications about eight, nine months ago."

"You sure?"

Kimball shrugged. "First victim I had was about four months ago. I'd have to look up the records on it."

"I think I'm going to need it. And anything else you have on the drug. Where it came from, how long it's been around, and anything special needed to produce it. Everything you have on it."

"Of course. I'll have it on the mainframe in an hour for you."

The computer to the side chirped and Kimball dropped his feet to the deck. He half turned, touched the keyboard, and watched as the screen brightened.

"Got the ID on the woman."

Brackett got up and moved around so that he could see. It showed a full face view of her that rotated slightly, first to the right and then to the left. She smiled self-consciously. The animation gave Brackett a much better feel for what she looked like living.

"Susan Sarah Bakker," said Kimball, reading aloud. "Born twenty-three years ago and trained as a computer repair technician." He glanced at Brackett. "Doesn't look like a computer technician."

Brackett watched as the preliminary information scrolled up. She had reported aboard about seven weeks earlier with a group of two dozen who had been assigned to the precinct.

She worked the swing shift in the computer repair shop, rarely having to leave there. Her quarters were with others of a similar work level, she stayed to herself, had no relatives on board, and no one seemed to know her very well.

"Place to start," said Brackett.

"I can get the autopsy file on the mainframe for you too," said Kimball.

"I'm not sure that it'll be necessary. The knife wounds killed her."

"Right. And her body showed almost no sign of deterioration from the drug. She just started using."

Stroking his chin, Brackett said, "Might help to find out how she got hooked."

"That's your job," said Kimball. He looked at the clock on the bulkhead near the hatch. "You ready for some lunch?"

"That always amazes me," said Brackett. "Cut up a body and then go eat lunch."

"Ah, my boy, you don't pay attention. I don't eat meat. Vegetables and fruits and sometimes eggs. No blood or gore to get in the way."

"Don't you ever have a craving for a thick steak?"

"Good God no! Not after what I've seen. Besides, where are you going to get a steak on the precinct?"

"Synthetic."

"Not the same," said Kimball. "It's just so much vegetable matter combined to look and taste like the real thing, but it's not. You can tell the difference. I prefer not to have my food masquerading as something that it's not. I prefer honesty."

"You're buying," said Brackett.

"Why? I'm the one who helped you. You should buy."

"But no one else wants to be seen with you," said Brackett. "Makes them uneasy."

"Okay," said Kimball, rising. "I'll buy."

Obo continued strolling the alien mall, watching a variety of beings, from the tall and humanoid to the short and unidentifiable. A precinct that traveled the stars had a need for a wide variety of accommodations, shops, outlets, and alien beings.

The brightly colored awning on a recessed shop caught his eye. He moved toward it and found that the way into the store was blocked by a rough wooden bar. Beyond it, the interior was dark and looked humid. There were huge trees and broad-leafed bushes that dripped into shallow pools.

The proprietor was a short scaly creature of a dark blue. He stood in knee-deep water, shuffling his feet to splash the water up onto his chest and back. He bent at the waist, cupped some water, and poured it over his head.

"You want?" he asked.

Obo shrugged, not sure of what he was doing. He stepped to the bar and felt the soft flow of the damp air. "Where are you from, old boy?"

"Zeta Reticuli."

"Never been there."

Bowing, the proprietor waved a hand. "We have much to offer."

Obo avoided stepping into shallow pools. Tau Ceti was a dry world with large sections bordering on arid. Obo didn't like to stand in water, avoided swimming, which he found to be ridiculous, and tried to stay away from worlds where the humidity was high and there were huge oceans, lakes, and rivers.

"Food?" asked Obo.

"Delicacies from home."

"Such as?"

The proprietor bent and scooped something from the water. Setting it on the bar, he said, "Auta."

It was an ugly, sluglike beast that looked fat and slimy. Obo wanted nothing to do with it as it crawled slowly toward the edge of the bar as if to drop back into the water.

"Pull the shell away from the back and eat."

"No, thank you," said Obo. "That all you have?"

"Many things. Have you been to Zeta Reticuli?"

"Nope," said Obo, thinking the creature didn't listen.

"We have everything here that you could find there. In the back is the gaming room. Four individuals, stripped, sitting in shallow pools, playing."

"You have everything?"

"Nothing illegal, of course."

"Thanks," said Obo.

He walked toward the next booth. There he saw a small, troll-like creature. The face looked as if it had been carved from old wood and the hands appeared to be gnarled roots. He sat behind a grindstone wheel that he was operating with a foot treadle.

Arranged on a standing piece of plywood were knives, hatchets, swords, and axes. There were practice swords and foils and axes made of wood.

"Hello," said the troll. "Do you see something that you like?"

"You sell weapons?"

"With the full approval of the administration of this precinct. Edged weapons for those who wish to develop a skill. It provides an opportunity for exercise."

Obo moved toward the wall. There were swords with long blades engraved with ornate designs. Others had curved blades and fancy hilts. And others that looked functional rather than decorative.

The troll appeared at his elbow. "An edged weapon is more personal than a gun."

"Are you advocating a way of thinking?"

"Oh, no. I'm merely pointing out the facts. Edged weapons have a variety of uses." He touched a small knife. "This can be used for carving, for food preparation, for decoration, or for protection."

"Do you sell many knives?"

"I make a meager living. Most of my time is taken in repair and in sharpening. There isn't much of a call for edged weapons in today's worlds. Everyone overlooks their value."

Obo stood in front of the display, searching for a weapon

that could have inflicted the wounds on the murder victims. The problem was that any sharp instrument could have been used and although the forensic pathologists might be able to identify in a gross sense the type of knife, he could not identify an individual weapon.

"You're a big strapping fellow," said the troll. "You look like you could use one of these with ease." He took down a broadsword. "Would you like to try it?"

"I don't believe so."

"Well, that's up to you. Something you wanted specifically?"

"No. I'm just looking. I don't get down here very often and I thought I would just see what was here." He thought for a moment. "Is there one species that seems more interested in knives than another?"

The troll put the sword back on display and sat down at his grindstone. He picked up a knife, began pumping away, and touched the knife blade against the wheel.

Obo turned and spotted a small case holding other knives. They had jewel-encrusted hilts, silver-inlaid hilts, and fancy curving blades. Small tags were attached to most of them showing that they were for sale.

"Knives have an universal appeal," said the troll finally. "All species come by to look at my weapons. Eventually everyone comes by my shop."

"You have records?"

The troll cocked his head to the side. "I have a listing for catalogs."

Obo filed the information and then turned. "Thanks for your time."

"I'll be here if you decide you need something."

Obo moved on, to a stall that held jewelry created from glass, from the Plexiglas used for the reinforced viewing ports, from gemstones picked up on a dozen different worlds, and to odds and ends found in the trash.

The proprietor of the shop was a long, thin being that might have been female. She wore a flowing robe of pale blue streaked with white. As Obo approached, she bowed slightly, letting her long blond hair hide her face.

"May I help you?" She lifted a hand revealing skin that was a bright orange.

"Just looking," said Obo. He noticed that many of the items could be used as weapons. They were long, pointed, and looked as if they were edged. A clever killer could buy one, hone the edge, and have a weapon that masqueraded as jewelry. Glass could be sharpened to an edge that rivaled and surpassed that of the finest surgical instruments. With laser tempering, the edge was stronger than some of those on metal blades.

He had only searched a couple of shops and already he realized that his task was impossible. There was no way for him to find the source of the weapon without having the weapon in hand. It could have been purchased on this level, could have been brought on board by any of the people assigned to the precinct, or could have even been made by the killer.

He touched one of the necklaces that held a pale yellow stone that looked like a narrow and pointed icicle. With only the tiniest modification, it could be turned into a weapon.

Without another word, he left the shop and moved to the center of the mall. He spotted a vacant bench and hurried toward it, sitting down. The mall wasn't crowded now. Too many people were at work. Later it would be packed.

He watched the few people walking around. No one there seemed to have a purpose. They were shoppers, out because they had nothing better to do. They walked slowly, staring at everything that was for sale. A few dickered with the shop owners, trying to talk them into some kind of a deal. Nothing seemed out of place.

Obo enjoyed watching others, seeing how they related in various environments. The diversity of the mall level made it an exciting assignment but he saw nothing that suggested the killer was there. No one with a haunted look, or who moved as if he had a mission. Nothing out of the ordinary.

Finally Obo stood up and headed back to the upper levels. Before he could do anything useful in the mall, he would need more information. He hoped that Brackett or Daily had learned something. If not, the investigation was going to take a long time.

10 | You Just Can't Believe Everything You Hear and Only Half of What You See

Brackett enjoyed the lunch with Kimball, only because Kimball refused to mention his work. Instead they talked of a dozen different things, never touching on the crimes that had been committed. Finished, Kimball returned to his office and Brackett headed into the upper levels.

When he reached his office, he found the note left by Daily. He read it quickly and then wadded it into a tiny ball. Suddenly he was angry at her. She shouldn't have entered into the undercover assignment without checking in with him. She was now out of touch, though he didn't think she was in danger. If he wanted, he could probably locate her in fifteen minutes using the computer systems and his friends.

Instead he typed Susan Sarah Bakker into his computer and sat back to read the entire file. But the preliminaries he'd seen in Kimball's office gave all the information. Susan Sarah Bakker had led an undistinguished life until she was murdered. That was the only thing out of the ordinary. He pulled up the identification of the section where she worked, the names of her fellow employees, and decided that the best thing he could do was walk down to see if someone could help him.

The computer repair shops were located on a corridor that had easy access to the mainframe. There were several of them, each specializing in specific aspects of computer repair. One dealt with hardware, another with soft, and a third with peripheries.

Brackett entered the first. It was a large room with workbenches bolted to the deck, high chairs surrounding tables, and a number of computers, both up and running and in pieces.

"Help you?" asked one of the men. He was young, with long hair, the beginnings of a mustache, and remnants of acne.

"You need a haircut," said Brackett.

"Why?"

"Doesn't the long hair get in the way of the work?"

"Nope. We don't need a sterile environment for the equipment. Little hair won't hurt, though we vacuum the cards before we reinsert them. If we need to, we wear hair nets, though it's none of your business."

Brackett waved a hand as if to wipe the slate clean. "Let me start again. I was just surprised because you have long hair."

"No problem. What can I do for you?"

"Do you know Susan Sarah Bakker?"

"Sure. Works next door. Went to lunch with her once in a while even. Nice lady though she stays to herself. Doesn't party with us."

"Seen her lately?"

The man put down his screwdriver. "What's going on here?"

"My name's Lieutenant Brackett."

"Cop."

"And I'm trying to get a line on this Bakker."

"She do something wrong?"

"No. It's routine." Brackett thought about it for a moment. Sometimes people clammed up when they learned that someone was dead. Sometimes they just clammed up fearing that the police would be up to no good, no matter what they were doing. He toyed with the idea of telling the man the truth and then rejected it, letting the silence between them grow.

The man finally spoke. "Haven't seen her in about a week or so. Course, that's not unusual either. If we're busy, or they are over there, we sometimes don't see each other regularly."

"What can you tell me about her?"

The man shrugged helplessly. "Not much really. Just came on board. Like I said, we went to lunch once or twice but nothing else."

"She tell you about herself?"

"Not that much. Say, there was one thing. She wasn't born on Earth."

"Why do you think that's important?"

"I don't know. I just thought it was interesting, I guess. She was human but not born on Earth. Most humans were born there."

"Friends?"

"Couple. You could ask them next door. They work with her. Probably know more about her."

"Anything unusual about her?"

Shaking his head, the man said, "No. Seemed like a nice woman. Good at her job and didn't complain. At least not so I'd know it."

"Okay," said Brackett. "Thanks."

He left and walked to the next shop. It was a carbon copy of the first. One woman stood as he entered and came toward him. "Can I help you?"

"You know Susan Sarah Bakker."

"Yeah." She frowned.

"You don't look happy."

"She left us hanging here. Hasn't been into work for a week so we have to pick up the slack. Who are you?"

"Lieutenant Brackett."

"Do you know where she is?"

Brackett ignored the question. Instead, he said, "What can you tell me about her?"

"She's a good worker when she shows up but the last two,

three weeks, she's been gone more than she's here. I went by her cabin, but her roommate hadn't seen her in a couple of days. She hasn't been sick. If she doesn't show up tomorrow or Wednesday, I'm going to have to report her."

That wasn't what Brackett wanted to hear. He wanted to know about the person. He wanted to see something of her rather than hear a complaint that she hadn't been to work lately.

"Do you like her?"

"Sure. She was nice enough. Stays to herself but does her work. She's a little wild once in a while. Likes to go dancing and once stayed out all night, coming here looking like something the cat dragged in." She laughed. "But stayed the day and completed everything. I thought she'd fade out but she didn't. Has a lot of energy."

"Friends with her?"

"I guess I was. We had drinks a couple of times. She went out with some of the others, but she didn't always jump into the games. Lots of times she stood on the sidelines and watched. She liked to go dancing and used the service club below. The Cat's Paw."

Brackett knew that he wasn't getting anywhere. He could spend a day putting together a profile that would tell him nothing that an experienced investigator with a lot less rank couldn't learn. He needed to search her quarters and find out if there was someone special she saw.

"Anything that you can tell me about her that you found . . . maybe a little odd?"

"No . . . She was a hard worker until the last few days. A quiet, sincere, dependable girl."

"Thanks," said Brackett. When they started repeating themselves, it meant that they knew nothing more to tell. He could have someone do the follow-ups later and then get it all into the computer.

Now was the time to search her cabin. See if something could be learned there.

• • •

Daily woke with a start, her neck twisted and aching and her mouth tasting as if it was filled with sand and mud. Her feet were cold and her eyes were blurry. She was not used to sleeping in a corridor with a dozen other people.

She looked to the right and found a man lying on his side, his knees drawn up nearly to his chest. His breathing was loud and rhythmic, telling her that he was asleep. One hand clutched the neck of an empty bottle that could have held any of a dozen different beverages, most of them filled with alcohol.

She stretched, felt her calf begin to cramp, and leaned forward to massage it. As she did, she noticed that her socks were dingy and then realized that she shouldn't have been able to see her socks.

Someone had stolen her shoes while she slept. She studied the people around her, searching their faces and then their feet, but her shoes were gone. Standing up with her back to the bulkhead, she wanted to scream.

A woman sitting opposite her said, "Got to be careful. New shoes. Somebody's gonna take them."

"You saw?"

"Yeah but I couldn't do a thing. She was bigger than me and had a knife. Cut the laces and slipped them off your feet as easy as pie."

"You could have stopped her."

"I didn't want to get cut. She had the look."

"What look?" Daily crouched down, a hand on her knee.

"Desperation. She was gonna take them shoes and that was it. If I opened my mouth, she'd have cut me. And you'd still have lost those shoes."

"Maybe not. Where'd she go?"

The woman shrugged, holding up her two dirty hands. "Take your choice. One way or t'other don't matter. She's long gone and so's your shoes."

Daily took a deep breath and slipped back to the deck, sitting there cross-legged. She felt a rumbling in her stomach that told her she was hungry but knew she couldn't just head up to the mall or the Cup and Hole to buy something. That would blow her cover.

"What you doing here?" asked the woman.

"What are any of us doing here?" responded Daily.

"I'm here because my old man found a younger and prettier woman to share his cabin. Now she doesn't have to work very hard and he takes care of her."

"So you could have gotten a job."

"Sure. As what? I was on the precinct because he was here. I was going to watch the kids we never had."

"There are training programs."

"They ask for qualifications," she said. "I got no skills at all."

The man stirred, sat up, and stretched his arms high above his head. He looked at the two women and said, "Tell her the truth, Sadie. You're as lazy as the rest of us."

"Not true. I tried but no one would give me a break."

"Not bad here," said the man. "No one freezes and no one starves. Sometimes we don't get to bathe and sometimes people steal the little we have, but it could be worse. At least we're not punching a time clock."

Daily looked at the man. "Everyone have that attitude?"

Sadie jumped in. "Hell no! Some have no other choice. There are rents to pay, food costs money. So do clothes and water and electricity. This ain't just a police precinct. It's a city with services that cost money or credit docked from your weekly pay. If you have a job."

"You want a job, Sadie, you just run on up to the mall and find yourself one. Plenty of them up there."

"Where do I stay tonight?" she asked. "I have to work the first week to get paid."

"Stay here and then, next week, find a cabin."

Sadie shook her head. "If it was only that easy." She turned on Daily. "I tried. I really tried, but there was nothing available for me. The shops are family run so there is no room for an outsider. The government jobs require skills but

I don't have any. Training programs don't pay if they exist at all. It's a vicious circle."

"So what do you do?" asked Daily.

"Drink," said the man, waving his empty bottle. "Drink when we have it. Or drugs. Anything to fill the time and make it a little easier."

"Drugs aren't the answer." She knew the moment she said it she shouldn't have. Preaching about drugs wouldn't get her into the circles she needed to penetrate.

But the man didn't seem to notice. "You ain't been down here long enough."

"Where do we get something to drink?" asked Daily.

"You have money?" asked the man.

"Don't tell him," warned Sadie. "He'll just steal it the first chance he gets. He's no good."

Sitting up straighter, he said, "I can show you where to get something to drink. Maybe a little more if you're interested in it."

"Okay," said Daily.

"Don't," said Sadie. "These people down here . . . some of them aren't really human. Nice girl like you, they'll be all over you in minutes."

"I can take care of myself." She stood up again and then looked down at her feet, wiggling her toes. "I'd like to get my shoes back."

"Course you would. Maybe we can find the woman who stole them. Maybe."

"And food?" asked Daily.

"You are a babe in the woods, aren't you?"

"How'd you end up down here?" asked Sadie.

Daily shrugged her shoulders and shook her head. "Boyfriend . . . found him in bed with my best friend."

"Good Christ," said Sadie. "You're a runaway. For God's sake, Zach, let her be. She'll get tired or hungry and go back where she belongs . . . Runaway. Sheet." She shook her head disapprovingly.

"Girl's got a right to do what she wants." He reached out

and took her elbow in an almost fatherly way. "I'll show you the ropes down here. Protect you."

For an instant Daily was going to pull away and then stopped herself. If she was going to be accepted, she needed a guide. She needed protective coloration and that was what Zach offered her. A way to slip into the inner reaches of the society without the weeks it would take by observation alone. And if Zach had ulterior motives, they wouldn't be anything that she couldn't handle.

They started toward the end of the corridor without a look back at Sadie. She stayed sitting on the deck, her mouth closed. She tried to give her warning and failed.

As they walked away, Daily asked, "How'd you end up down here?"

"Just lucky, I guess."

11 | Home Is Where You Find It

The cabin was not what he had expected. Raised on a generation of vidcomedies, and having no practical experience with young women, Brackett didn't know what he had expected, exactly. Maybe something with clothes scattered on the deck, the pull-down bunks unmade, and fast-food containers growing a wide range of biological products.

Instead, he found a cabin that was almost Spartan. There was nothing on the deck that didn't belong there. Two pairs of shoes stood in the corner. The bunks had been lifted out of the way, and the clothes were either packed away in the drawers, or hanging off to one side where they should have been.

Brackett stood at the hatch, his back to it, and searched it with his eyes but found nothing unusual. He took a step in, reached out, and ran a hand through the tiny closet, looking at the clothes hanging there. Amateurs, not knowing that every hiding place had already been thought of and that there were no clever hiding places, often packed the pockets with valuables from currency to drugs. But there was nothing to be found here. No drugs, no cash, no costume jewelry that was valuable only to its owner.

He checked the deck under the clothes, checked the shoes, ran a hand over the shelf and then down the bulkhead, searching for anything that didn't belong. Nothing.

The bunks, the drawers, the little desk, were clean too.

Nothing that shouldn't have been there was there. No sign of anything out of the ordinary. Maybe a few too many clothes but then, there weren't too many things that a young woman with room and board provided would need to buy.

He yanked down one of the bunks, felt along the side, lifted the paper-thin mattress and searched, but nothing was hidden there except a single letter postmarked Sirius Four. It was a grotesquely embarrassing love letter that spelled out clinically everything sexually the young man wanted to do. From the smudges, it looked as if it had been read dozens of times.

He put it back, smoothed down the mattress, and then sat down, feet flat on the floor. There was absolutely nothing in the cabin that would tell him why Susan Sarah Bakker had been carved up below.

Taking a deep breath, he stood and turned slowly, examining the cabin a final time. Nothing. No clues. No signs. Nowhere for him to go.

As he moved toward the hatch, it irised open and a young woman stepped through. She was dressed in a skintight jumpsuit that did nothing to conceal the fact she was female. When she saw Brackett, she didn't jump back, didn't scream, and in fact didn't react except to push a lock of dark hair away from her eyes.

The silence between them grew but Brackett didn't speak. He stared at her hard, into her eyes, trying to get some kind of reaction. His clothing didn't mark him as a cop, and he'd been told by friends that he looked less like a cop than some of the people he had arrested. He liked the protective coloration and cultivated it.

The woman finally broke the staring contest and moved toward the closet, grabbing a hanger. Without looking, she asked, "What do you want?"

Brackett noted that she hadn't asked who he was. That meant she thought she knew. Maybe she had recognized him, but he wasn't going to give her the benefit of the doubt. Let her make a mistake if that was what she was going to do.

"Sue isn't here," she said.

"Where?"

The girl shrugged her shoulders and then turned to face him. Her hand posed at the top of her jumpsuit, over the Velcro fastenings. She pulled it down with the sound of ripping cloth. The material spread apart showing off her body but revealing nothing that was considered private.

"I haven't seen her in a week. You'll have to go elsewhere to find her."

"Where?"

"How in the hell should I know? It's not my business. Now I want you to get out of here before I call a cop."

Brackett didn't move and didn't speak.

"Look, I wasn't into that and told her it would get her into trouble, but she wouldn't listen. She knew better than everyone else. She was a big girl. I had nothing to do with it."

Brackett knew that anything he asked, unless he guessed exactly right, would shut down the flow of information. Sometimes there was no better interrogation technique than keeping his mouth shut and letting the subject talk.

"She's been gone for a week and I don't know where. That's it."

"Boyfriend?" said Brackett.

"Louis something," she said, waving a hand. "I don't know anything else. Sometimes he's at the Cat's Paw."

"You know him?"

"He's been here once or twice."

"Get dressed. You're going with me."

"No I'm not. I have nothing to do with her use. I told her the stuff would kill her. Now you get out or I'm calling the cops."

Brackett reached into his pocket and took out his badge and holopicture ID. "I'm the cops."

She looked at the badge and ID and the strength seemed to drain from her body. She took a step to the right and sat down on the edge of the bunk. "Christ."

"What's your name?"

"Linda Pierson."

"Well, Linda, you and I are going to have a very nice, long talk."

"I have nothing to say to you."

Brackett grinned and said, "This is a sovereign state. The rules of evidence, the rules of interrogation, the rules of the accused, are different from those on many planets. I tell you this so that you know that I can take you to a holding cell and keep you there for either of two reasons. All I have to say is that you are a material witness in the crime of murder and you have no rights. Or I can say that I believe you are involved in the crime of murder on the precinct, and your rights evaporate. I hold all the cards."

"But . . ." She wanted to protest that it didn't work that way because she'd seen all the viddramas about criminals and murder but she wasn't sure of the law. Fright had yet to wash over her.

Brackett wiped his hand over his face. He took a step toward the girl and looked down at her. "I want to know what happened in the last few weeks. I want to know who you thought I was and what you thought she was into."

For a moment Pierson sat quietly and then it began to dawn on her. There was nothing she could say or do. She studied the deck and then her shoulders began to shake. Looking up, she said, "I don't want to get Sue into trouble."

"Sue's already in trouble and there is nothing that you could say that would make it worse for her. It's as bad as it gets."

"Is she in custody?"

"You could say that. Now I want an answer to my questions." He'd let his voice soften a bit. The hard-nosed act was one that he could return to if she began to clam up. At the moment it appeared that she was ready to spill her guts.

"There have been a couple of men by here in the last few days demanding money. I told them that I didn't owe them anything but they insisted on payment, if not from Sue, then from me. Sue owes them the money."

"What men?"

"I don't know. They just come in and ask. Or did ask. Now they demand. Either Sue has to pay them or they expect me to."

"What was she into?"

The woman looked up then. She was unaware that the top of her jumpsuit had pulled open wider and suddenly the view had improved. Brackett knew that it wasn't a trick to seduce him because there were no other cues. Her eyes were shiny but not with lust. She was on the verge of tears, frightened that she was going to end up in custody.

"Something new. A drug of some kind. I don't know much about it. She met Louis at the Cat's Paw and he gave it to her. After that she'd do anything to get more. Anything at all."

"Descriptions of the men who came by here."

"I don't . . . average. Light hair, strong-looking. Not overly tall or heavy. Nothing unusual about them except their attitude. Rough. Mean."

"Would you recognize them?"

"Maybe . . ."

"Get dressed," said Brackett. "We're going to the Cat's Paw for the evening."

"I really should . . ."

"This is not a date nor is it a request. I'm in the middle of an investigation."

"What about Sue?"

"She can't get into any more trouble than she is already in."

Together they walked down a dimly lighted corridor. Daily had not asked for Zach's last name. There were too many people in the lower reaches. They couldn't all be run-aways and dropouts. Some of them had to have sneaked on board.

"Don't mind Sadie," said Zach. "She hates all men since

her old men threw her out. Figures that all we've got on our minds is sex and free rides."

"You can't blame her."

"Hell, maybe she was such a bitch that her old man had to throw her out."

"And maybe he was an asshole."

"Maybe."

They came to a fork in the corridor and took the left one. A few feet later they found a stairway and used it to head deeper into the ship. It was nearly pitch-black, but the edges of the step were illuminated so that no one tripped. Zach put a hand on Daily's arm as if to help her down. When they reached the bottom, he kept it there.

He led her into another corridor. This one was wide but the bulkheads were covered with pipes and wires and the lights were covered with small wire cages so that the bulbs were protected. No one had wasted time, effort, or money on esthetics.

"Almost there," said Zach, finally removing his hand.

Daily noticed that she could still feel it, almost as if it had infected her. She decided that she didn't like the man at all and that it might be time to get the hell out of there.

"We've got a meeting place. Invite those we want to join. Food, warmth, and friendship."

They reached a hatch and Zach knocked on the bulkhead. Three short quiet taps and then a louder one. He leaned close and said, "Zach Peabody."

The hatch irised slightly and a man stuck his head out. "Who's she?"

"Friend."

"Okay." The head disappeared and the hatch opened the rest of the way.

The interior of the cabin was dim, large, and warm. People were scattered around the deck, some of them lying on their backs, some of them sitting, and some of them eating. Three couples, in various locations, were engaging in sex, oblivious to those around them, a few who were watching.

Peabody moved to the right and grabbed a bottle from a box on the floor. He opened it and drank from it, wiping his lips on the back of his hand. Then, pointing at Daily, he said, "I brung her down here because she needs something to eat."

"She know the rules?"

"Nope," said Peabody.

Daily stood rooted to the spot just inside the hatch, her eyes locked on the three couples. A woman who was on top of a man threw her head back and began to wail, first low, deep in her throat, and then louder. She seemed to lift herself up and then collapsed forward, the breath rasping in her throat.

Peabody, his eyes on the couple, approached Daily and handed her a bottle. "Little beer. Tonight's free but tomorrow you have to pull your weight."

Daily took the bottle but didn't drink from it. "Pull my weight?"

"We pool our resources here. You get something from a shop owner, you bring it down here. We all share. You have a bad day, there's still food."

"That all that's required?"

Peabody, still watching the couples, said, "That's all that's required. There are other activities, but participation is voluntary." Grinning, he added, "But some of it is a great deal of fun."

"Okay," said Daily. She took a sip of the beer. It was warm.

Peabody pointed at a spot on the deck. "Have a seat. We're all friends here. No pressure because that's what we were all getting away from. Pressure of the job or to perform or to produce. Here there is no pressure. You join in if you want. No one has any secrets."

"I can see that."

Peabody moved closer to her. "One big happy family," he said. "Helping one another."

"Sure."

They had wandered the lower regions of the precinct for more than five hours before they picked up a lead. Two men stood close together in the entrance to a stairway. They spoke in low tones and one man handed the other something. The seller then handed a small, clear envelope to the buyer.

"There you go," said one of the spies. "There's a deal going down."

The buyer and seller separated, one of them hurrying down the stairs and the other down the corridor.

"Which one do you want to follow?"

"Man going down. He's got the goods."

As soon as the seller was out of sight, the two men hurried after the buyer. At the top of the stairs they stopped long enough to make sure that the buyer wouldn't see them. Satisfied that it was clear, they rushed down the stairs.

They reached the corridor and saw the buyer as he dodged into a cabin about fifty meters away. They waited but no one else appeared and no one exited.

Looking at his watch, the leader said, "They should be well under by now."

"We kill them all again?"

"It's the only way. They'll never understand anything else. Make it deadly and they'll stop. Let them know that they'll die violently and they'll quit. It's retribution for preying on others."

"I suppose."

The leader took out his knife and examined the blade, touching the edge of it with the ball of his thumb. The knife was still razor-sharp.

They reached the cabin and opened the hatch. Four people were inside, all of them on the deck. They had used the drug just purchased and were almost unconscious.

"Seems wrong."

"So's destroying the body with drugs. So's stealing to support the habit. One way or another these people are going to die shortly. What difference does it make?"

"None."

"Then let's do it."

12 | When All Else Fails, Scream and Shout

The Cat's Paw was crowded and noisy and dark. There was a bar in the rear but most of the patrons were at small tables that ringed the dance floor, or out dancing, bouncing and gyrating to the heavy metal being pumped through the speakers. Colored lights flashed in time to the music creating a hypnotic effect that wasn't lost on Brackett. He knew that it was designed to keep the people there, drinking the alcohol so that the owner could make a pile of money.

Brackett took Pierson by the elbow and pulled her into the club. The driving beat of the music gave him a headache but he ignored it, pushing his way across the dance floor, toward the only vacant table he could see. Letting go of Pierson, he dropped into a chair and waved her into the other.

Leaning across it, her elbows propped on the center of it, she shouted, "This is no good."

"Why?"

"Too early. No one'll be here yet."

"Then enjoy the music. If you see Louis, or anyone else who knows Sue, you let me know."

She turned and watched the people as they danced. She kept her eyes moving, searched the entire mob, and then shook her head. "Nobody here."

"You said it was early."

"Yeah. Will you buy me something to drink?"

Brackett grinned. "I think we can afford something as long as we don't get too exotic."

Pierson waved a waitress over and got what she wanted. Sipping it, she surveyed the dancers again. "I don't suppose that you'd care to dance," she said.

"Nope. I haven't had enough to drink yet. I need two or three before I feel comfortable enough."

"Got to dance when you come here," said Pierson. "It's like an unwritten law."

"Can't enforce unwritten laws. If it's not written it has no teeth."

A young man appeared and leaned close to Pierson. He whispered something to her. She shook her head and pointed at Brackett.

"Oh, your father doesn't want you to date," he said.

"No," said Brackett, "I don't want her to have anything to do with assholes."

"You calling me an asshole?"

"Nope," said Brackett. "I said I don't want her to have anything to do with assholes."

"Then you are."

"You're making the determination. I merely set up the criterion."

"If you're looking for a fight, mister . . ."

"What is with you people? Come down here for fun and then want to pick a fight."

"Chicken?"

Now Brackett laughed. "Fight's the last thing you want. Take my word for it."

Pierson raised a hand and touched the man on the chin, forcing him to turn his head toward her. When she had his attention, "Leave it alone. You don't understand. Maybe I'll dance with you later."

He hesitated, shifting his eyes from Brackett to Pierson, and then said, "Okay. Later."

As he disappeared, Brackett said, "I can never understand that."

"You challenged him," said Pierson.

"No, he started it. He appeared here, trying to take on the older, dominant male so that the young female would become his. Standard tactics in baboon troops and with chimpanzees, but you would think humans would have outgrown that."

"You called him an asshole."

Brackett laughed again. "Because he challenged me with the crack about being your father. See, even I am not immune to our heritage."

Before she could answer, Brackett stood up and lifted a hand. As Obo approached, Brackett asked, "Just how in the hell did you find me?"

"Ship's sensors," said Obo. "I asked for the location of the various constables and by process of elimination was able to find you, old boy."

"I didn't want to be found."

"Then you should have let the computer know that you were working undercover."

"No," said Brackett. "Not undercover, but working." He held a hand out to the woman. "This is Linda Pierson. She's assisting me for the moment."

"Ms. Pierson," said Obo, bowing slightly.

"Now, what's the tragedy this time," asked Brackett.

Glancing at the woman, Obo hesitated. Brackett caught that and stepped away from the table. Obo leaned close and tried to whisper though the band was making so much noise that it would be impossible to be overheard.

"We've another one."

"One?"

"Murder. Same basic MO as the others. Captain Carnes has requested that you meet him in his office. I'm afraid that he was more than a little upset."

"I'm not surprised," said Brackett. "Carnes was born upset and hasn't improved." Moving back to the table, Brackett told Pierson, "I'm afraid that I've been called away."

"Too bad."

"I'll take you back to your cabin if you like."

"Now that I'm here, I think I'll stay."

"Fine. If you see Sue's boyfriend, I would appreciate it if you could get a last name and an occupation from him."

"I don't understand this," she said. "Why don't you get it from Sue. She'd know all about him." Then the color drained from her face and her eyes widened. "She's dead, isn't she?"

"I'm . . ."

"You answer my question."

Brackett slipped into the chair opposite her and said, "I'm very sorry, but yes, she is."

"Oh, God." She looked up at the lights overhead, blinking her eyes rapidly. "You're sure?"

"I'm afraid so. No question about it."

"How?"

Brackett shook his head. "We're investigating. That's why we'll need your help."

She wiped her eyes and then picked up her drink. She drained it and slammed it to the table. The music died at that moment and the dancers began drifting from the floor.

"You should have told me earlier."

"If you'd like to go back to your cabin."

"Yes," she said, nodding numbly. "Yes."

"Obo, please tell Captain Carnes I'll be up to see him as quickly as possible."

"Certainly, but the captain is going to be less than thrilled."

Brackett stood again and walked around so that he could assist Pierson. As they left the Cat's Paw, he realized that he could have handled that better. There had been no reason to tell her the truth in the club. He should have taken her outside before telling her about her roommate.

"Is there anything I can do?" he asked as they walked toward the lift.

"Haven't you done enough?"

"I suppose so."

• • •

Carnes didn't wait for Brackett to get the hatch closed before he exploded. He jumped from behind his desk, pointed a finger at Brackett, and yelled, "When I tell you I want you to report, it doesn't mean at your convenience."

Brackett let the hatch iris shut and moved closer to the desk.

Carnes leaned forward, both hands clenched in fists, and rested his knuckles on his desk. "Just where in the hell do you get off in interpreting my instructions."

In a reasonable voice, Brackett said, "I was involved with the investigation . . ."

"I know what you were doing. You were in the Cat's Paw on a date. During duty hours."

"No, sir," said Brackett. "I was attempting to find a suspect with the assistance of a civilian. The only information I had was that the suspect would be at the Cat's Paw."

"I don't want to hear your feeble excuses." Carnes's face had changed from red to purple. His voice had risen in pitch so that it was getting difficult to understand him. "I have a job to do here and you're supposed to be assisting, not taking women out in the middle of the afternoon."

Brackett knew that it would do no good to speak now. Carnes had made up his mind. Brackett had been caught having a good time when he was supposed to be on duty. Carnes wouldn't believe that he had been working no matter what evidence he presented.

"While you were having a good time, things have been happening. We have more dead. Four more people killed in the same fashion as the others."

"When?"

"Teams are on the scene now. I had expected you to take charge there, but I've Sergeant Gordon down there. He'll report to us." Carnes was calming down, his voice returning to normal.

Brackett looked at the chairs for the visitors but decided

he'd stand until invited to sit. There was nothing for him to do but stand and wait for Carnes to continue.

There was one thing that bothered him about the investigation. Although he was in overall charge, he had to spend time with the brass, explaining the progress or lack of it to them. But the real problem was that the on-site team, the first people there, were never the same. Each had been taken by a different sergeant. There should be coordination so that the same people arrived. It would give the investigation a continuity that it didn't have at the moment.

Carnes continued to rant, and shaking his head as if he couldn't believe the stupidity. "This has been going on for several days. What have you learned?" he demanded.

"Little," said Brackett. "We've identified two of the victims and are working to learn more about them."

"Two!" roared Carnes. "Why aren't there IDs on all of them?"

"That's the question," said Brackett. "I've had Obo and others going through the computer records, but there seem to be ways to gain access to the precinct without finding your way into the computer records."

"Bullshit!" said Carnes. "You do not get on here without going through checks."

"We might want to believe that," said Brackett, "but it doesn't seem to be true. The medical examiner and his people have been unable to identify the bodies because they don't show up in the computer files."

"I want those records checked again."

"Of course."

"What have you learned from the two you ID'ed?"

"That's what I was working on." Brackett explained that he had looked into the background of Susan Sarah Bakker but had yet to find anything that would explain why she had been found slaughtered on the lower levels of the precinct. There were some aberrations in her background. And, of course, Daily was working, but she had learned nothing yet.

Brackett didn't bother to mention that she had not reported in.

Carnes wiped a hand over his face and then smoothed down his thinning hair. He dropped back into his chair. "You don't know the pressure I'm under here. We can solve crimes on any planet in the galaxy but we can't solve one on our own precinct. Everyone is beginning to look incompetent."

Brackett took a deep breath. "We have only been working on this for a couple of days. It takes time to build the file so that we can find the perpetrator."

"I didn't ask for excuses," said Carnes. "I want results and I want them now."

"What would you suggest I do that we haven't done?"

"Don't take that tone with me," snapped Carnes. His voice rising again, he said, "I'm not one of your flunkies. I know what's going on. What you should have done, after the second set of murders, was go into the lower levels with armed officers and run everyone out of there. If they don't congregate, then there will be no targets."

Brackett had to agree with the philosophy but knew that it wouldn't answer the bigger question of who was committing the crimes and certainly wouldn't stop them. He could take out all the targets, or try, but the killer would keep on operating, maybe hiding out until the people began to filter back down.

"Well?"

"We could do that."

"Lieutenant, that wasn't a request or a suggestion. It was an order. I want those people out of there. I want them identified. And if they aren't in the computers, if they aren't authorized on the precinct, I want them removed. There will be no more crimes like those."

There was nothing for Brackett to say other than "Yes, sir."

"You get what you need, manpower and equipment, but you get those people rounded up. The holding cells can be utilized for this. I want to know the names of every one of them and I want to make sure that none of them are released until we have the killer in custody."

"If the killer is one of them . . ."

"Don't hand me that. The killer will be found down there. No law-abiding citizen could do anything like that. Now, do you have any questions?"

Brackett shook his head.

"Then you have twelve hours to finish this task. Now get the hell out of here."

Brackett stood and retreated quickly. The plan was the dumbest thing he'd ever heard. It would not solve the crimes but it would drain manpower away from what needed to be done and that would let the killer bury himself. With the cops busy down below, the killer didn't have to worry about them chasing him. Cops arresting people in the lower levels couldn't be investigating the crimes as they should be and Brackett didn't like that at all.

13 | Sometimes You Just Have to Kick the Shit Out of Them to Get Their Attention

Brackett returned to his office, punched up his display on his computer, and then ignored it. Instead he sat there thinking about what Carnes had just said. Carnes, as a police official, should understand the problems with finding a killer who chose his victims at random. And Carnes, as a police official, should have known that rousting people was not the way to conduct an investigation.

The logistics of the problem were simple. Two dozen officers, probably in riot gear, moving through the corridors, chasing out those who lived there. Those who resisted would be arrested and taken to holding cells. Those who got out would be allowed to escape. He didn't need twelve hours to plan the operation. Maybe thirty minutes.

Brackett rocked back in his chair and lifted his feet, propping them on the desk near the computer screen. There was something going on here that he didn't understand. Unseen forces were at work, causing problems. They were directing the investigation into areas where it didn't belong.

Carnes should have realized that by learning more about the victims, he might be able to learn a little about the killer. He had been trying to do that when he was pulled from the investigation. It could be coincidence, especially with another set of murders, but since he wasn't required at the scene, he should have been left to follow his lead.

He dropped his feet back to the deck and punched up the communications and asked for the medical examiner.

Kimball appeared and said, "I was just on my way out. Make it snappy."

"Nice to talk to you too."

"What do you need, Loot?"

"You know anything about the new crimes?"

"On my way to learn about them. Preliminaries, from the officers on the scene, suggest that it is just like the others. You going to be down there?"

"Carnes has other plans for me."

Kimball shrugged. "What can I tell you?"

"I need a full report as soon as you have it. You going to try another Steelman?"

"We've got it. Anything else?"

"No."

"See you." The screen darkened.

Brackett stood up and thought about heading down, but he'd be getting a full report. With holo, video, and Steelman, there was no reason for him to see the crime scene now. He could call it up later.

Obo appeared but didn't say anything. He stood silently, not wanting to interrupt.

"What?" asked Brackett.

"Sergeant Daily," he said.

Brackett looked up at him. "Sergeant Daily is continuing in her undercover assignment." He was quiet and then added, "But I understand. We haven't heard from her."

"So we should go to find her, old girl."

Brackett grinned at that. Obo's English continued to improve but sometimes he made silly mistakes. In answer, he said, "Yeah, we need to go get her. But I've got to get some things done first. Get some people working."

"I'll wait right here."

Brackett ran a fingernail down the list of duty officers and then punched a code into the commo. The screen brightened. "Sergeant Walsh here."

"Lieutenant Brackett."

"Yes, sir. I recognize you."

"I want surveillance on Linda Pierson. She is the cabin mate of a murdered woman. I want to know where she goes, what she does, and who she does it with."

"Yes, sir. Starting when."

"Ten minutes ago would have been good. Thirty minutes from now will be fine."

"Yes, sir."

When the screen went blank, Brackett dialed another number. It was answered, "Computing."

"Got a major problem for you."

The young woman grinned and said, "That's what we're here for. To solve your major problems."

"We have learned that there are a number of people on the precinct who are not listed in the normal channels. I want a cross-check made and I want a list of everyone on the precinct."

"Everyone?"

"Right. Everyone," said Brackett.

"Why?"

"Because," said Brackett. He didn't want to explain it to her. In fact, didn't think that it was necessary to explain it to her.

"There are more than fifteen thousand people assigned to the precinct."

Brackett sat back and rubbed his eye, trying to figure out exactly what he needed.

"Medical examiner has asked us to perform a similar task," said the woman.

"What are you doing?"

"Cross-checking the boarding manifests with the departing crew. We're also checking the death certificates, requests for occupancy, tenant statements, pay records, and census forms with the manifests to see which names pop up or fail to pop up. It's a complex task."

"How long?"

"We've been working on it for two days, but you have to understand the vast volume of information that we have to search. Everyone has records and everyone is keeping records of everything. The computer is working as fast as it can."

"Plug Susan Sarah Bakker into your computer."

"Why?"

"She's one of those that has—what?—dropped out. See if that clues you into where to look."

"Sure, but it's going to take a while. You wouldn't believe the data being stored."

Brackett was sure that he would, but he didn't want to know about it. If he learned exactly what was held in the various computer banks he was sure that he would be frightened. It would indicate that a computer freak with a mean streak could learn everything he wanted and use it. Brackett preferred to live in his world thinking that there were things that no one would be able to find. He knew it wasn't true, he just liked the warm, fuzzy feeling.

"When you get something, could you let me know?"

"Sure. Dr. Kimball said to put you on the distribution list."

"Thanks."

As Brackett signed off, Obo said, "I finished searching for an outlet for knives. Nothing to help us there."

Brackett made a note. He knew that it was a long shot at best. Edged weapons weren't like the old firearms. There were distinct signatures left by the barrels of firearms but a knife blade wasn't distinctive. The ME might be able to tell the kind, if it was a butcher knife or a hunting knife or a pocket knife. He might be able to learn if it was a Randall or a Gerber or a Ginzu. But unless they found the specific knife and could use blood residue to tie it to the crimes, it made no difference what kind it was.

"Are we going to go find Sergeant Daily?"

Brackett turned off the computer. "I think that it's time that we went to find her."

● ● ●

Daily awoke with a start. Someone was tugging at the buttons of her shirt. She slapped at the hands as she opened her eyes and stared into the leering face of Zach Peabody.

"Just what in the hell do you think you're doing?"

"Take it easy," said Peabody. He rocked back on his heels and studied her. "It's nothing you haven't done before."

"But I say when," said Daily. She felt the anger burn through her. "Just who in the hell do you think you are?"

"We all cooperate down here. We share everything. It is the only way to survive."

"Crap," said Daily, pushing herself back against the bulkhead. She noticed that her jacket, which she had rolled up for a pillow was gone. As was everything else that she had brought with her. Everything that hadn't been fastened to her, and if Peabody hadn't been clumsy, they'd probably have gotten most of that.

"You don't understand how it is," said Peabody. "You came down only yesterday. You haven't felt real hunger. You haven't felt real despair as the life you thought you'd have was ripped away by the bureaucrats."

"What life?" asked Daily contemptuously.

"I had plans once but they gave the job to a younger man who had political connections. Fucking Star Cops. You have pull and you rise right up the ladder but if you don't . . . nothin'."

"So you dropped out?"

"Why the fuck not?" He stayed where he was, crouching in front of her, watching her closely, his hands inches from her shirt buttons. "No more pressure down here. No one caring." He rocked forward on his knees and tentatively reached out toward her shirt.

"Keep your hands off me."

"I told you that we share down here. You got one thing that everyone'll want. Make your life easier."

"Not with you."

"Not much you can do about it."

"You take a lot for granted, friend. There're people all around me."

Peabody waved a hand. "They don't care. Leave them alone and they're happy. Sheep. Do what they're told. Life throws them a curve and they get out."

"You're no better," said Daily. She shifted slowly, carefully, trying to get her feet under her so that she could stand up.

As Daily pulled away from him, Peabody followed, keeping his face only inches from hers, his eyes locked on hers. "Better get used to it."

Daily reached out suddenly and shoved Peabody away. He fell back as she stood up. As he scrambled around, she snapped a foot out, catching him under the jaw. His head snapped back as pain shot up her leg. He fell to the deck and rolled to his right, moaning low in his throat.

"You stupid bitch," said Peabody, leaping to his feet. "You think you're better than us?" He got to his feet and stood between her and the hatch, his hands out as if he expected to grab her.

Around them others were beginning to take interest. They slipped right or left, out of the way, but no one offered her any help. Any diversion, no matter what, was considered major entertainment.

"Back off," said Daily. "You don't know what you're getting yourself into."

"It's going to happen," said Peabody. "You might as well enjoy it."

"Okay, I warned you," said Daily. She had been backing up, trying to avoid the fight, but Peabody would give her no choice. He was going to push it to the end.

Suddenly she stepped forward and that surprised him. In that moment of confusion, she kicked again, bringing her knee up sharply. Peabody turned at the last instant, but he wasn't quite quick enough. He took a glancing blow as fire exploded into his crotch and icy fingers grabbed his belly.

But he didn't fall as she expected. He grabbed her, hands on her arms, pinning them to her sides, pulling her toward him.

Daily allowed that, but then twisted around so that he was facing her back. She stomped his foot, bringing her heel down on his toes. At the same time she slammed her fist into his crotch. As his grip weakened, she whirled again and struck at his eyes with her fists, thumbs extended. She felt them slide in as the man screamed in pain, falling back to the deck.

Breathing heavily, sweat drenching her, she lifted a foot to stomp his throat. Peabody, unaware of that, rolled away from her, his hands over his eyes and his knees hiked up. He moaned low in his throat, sounding as if he could no longer scream.

Daily suddenly realized that she would kill Peabody if she stomped him. She put her foot on the deck and then wiped the sweat from her face. She glanced to the right and left, but no one was moving.

"Anyone else?" she asked breathlessly. "Anyone?"

"You didn't have to beat him so badly," said someone quietly.

She whirled toward the speaker. "Why the hell not?" she demanded. "He's lucky I didn't kill him."

Another voice said, "We'd better get him up to the hospital."

Daily nodded and pointed. "Go ahead. Get him the hell out of here."

"You'd better go yourself," said the leader. "You don't belong."

"Yeah," said Daily. "I don't understand how you can steal from one another and let slime like this in here. I'll gladly get out."

She looked around but no one was moving. No one was offering to help her or to give her stuff back to her. She stepped over Peabody and walked to the hatch. As it irised open, she stepped out, into the corridor. As she walked toward the stairs, she realized that she had learned almost nothing except that humans always let someone lead them, no matter what the circumstances, and that they still didn't want to get involved. She learned nothing about the society that would help identify the killers, and in that sense, she failed.

14 | Violence Sure Put an End to World War II

Carnes had stayed in his office after Brackett was gone, and watched as the holographic sun slipped across the sky to vanish behind the holographic city telling him that evening was coming. He had thought that he would stay in the office and let others report to him, but the inspector had called and had wanted to know what was happening. Even though Carnes had shifted the blame to Brackett, he was still on the hot seat. He would have to do something.

Finally he decided that he would have to go down and see how the investigation was progressing. There was nothing else that he could do.

In the outer office he told his artificial secretary in her short skirt and a nearly invisible blouse that he would be back later and to take messages. The advantage of an artificial secretary was that she never required a coffee break, never took a long lunch, or any lunch for that matter, and that she would be there no matter what time Carnes returned.

He hurried to the lift, punched the buttons, and rode down, trying not to think about what he was going to see. Dead and bloody bodies were not his favorite thing and during his rise through the hierarchy he hadn't had to look at many.

When the doors opened, he stepped out and saw that the corridor was loaded with people—workers going home, others about to report to duty, people shopping for dinner or clothes or just looking for a good time.

Ignoring them, he hurried down the corridor, took the stairs lower, and searched for the crowd. They were clustered at the far end, around a hatch. As he approached, an officer broke from the pack and moved to intercept him and then recognized him.

"Sergeant Gordon?"

"He's inside with Dr. Kimball."

"Who are all these other people?"

"Crowd control, investigators, medical examiner and his people, photographers . . ."

"Okay," said Carnes. He stepped around the officer and stared into the cabin. The four bodies were sprawled where they had fallen. Blood had pooled on the deck, but it had also splattered the bulkheads. Crouching over one of the dead was the ME with the Steelman in his hand.

Carnes moved in and asked, in a voice that was louder than it had to be, "You getting anything?"

Kimball jumped and nearly lost his grip on the Steelman. "Christ, you don't have to shout."

"Sorry."

Placing the probe between the victim's eyes, Kimball watched the tiny monitor. He shifted it around but the readings he had been getting had faded.

"Screwed that one up, Carnes."

"Bull. Just asked a question. You know the Steelman isn't all that reliable."

"I don't need you coming in here to tell me that. And I don't need you cluttering the area with spurious psychic energy," said Kimball.

"Sorry."

He shook his head like a doctor who had just lost a patient. "Nothing now."

"You get anything at all?"

"We'll have to see, but I think it was too cluttered with a drug-induced fog. If there was anything, we'll be very lucky."

"I'll want a complete report."

"As soon as we get it."

Carnes turned his attention to one of the examiners who was looking at the wounds of one of the dead. He knelt beside her and said, "What have you got?"

"Not much. Sharp instrument. See the way the skin has pulled back. Very sharp. The interesting thing is that all the wounds are slash type. No stabbing this time."

"That significant?"

She shrugged. "Who knows? Before there was a combination of slash and stab. No defensive wounds again. That tells us something."

Carnes stood up and moved back toward the hatch. He turned, leaned against the bulkhead, and watched as the others went about their jobs. He scanned the deck, the bodies, everything, looking for clues that the others might have missed, but saw nothing. He was accomplishing nothing there except getting in the way.

"Sergeant Gordon?"

"Yes, sir."

"I'm going back to my office. When you finish here, I want a full report."

"Yes, sir."

Daily walked slowly through the corridors in the lower levels. Occasionally she saw someone who had taken up space in an alcove or in the recessed entrance to one of the cabins. More people congregated in the lowest levels where the majority of the crew, the workers, the cops, everyone on the precinct rarely made their way.

She glanced back over her shoulder but didn't see anyone chasing her. No one cared that she had left the area and were probably happy that she was gone.

At the lift, she stopped and then turned. The undercover assignment was blown. There was no way that she could remain down there and be accepted at face value. The story of what she'd done would make its way through the levels until everyone was aware of it.

The doors opened but she didn't enter. Instead she stepped

back so that the heat sensor would lose sight of her and allow the doors to close again. Maybe the assignment wasn't ruined. Maybe it suddenly became easier because everyone would know that she wasn't someone to be pushed around. She could take care of herself and wasn't timid about it.

For a moment she stood there, looking back the way she had come. Maybe she should return and find Sadie. The old woman had warned her about Peabody, had tried to help her, but she hadn't listened. Maybe that was the key to the whole thing.

She walked back down the corridor and then spotted a woman lying just inside a cabin. The door had been propped open so that the dim lights of the corridor would bleed into the cabin. In that half-light, she recognized one of her shoes.

"Son of a bitch," she said and stepped into the cabin. The sleeping woman didn't move.

There was no one else in the cabin. The woman was lying with her head in the shadows but her feet were in the light. She noticed that the laces of the shoes were different than the ones she'd had in them. The thief had cut the laces to get the shoes and had to replace them.

Daily couched there, staring down at the shoes. It wasn't as if she needed them. In her cabin far above were more shoes. Most of the corridors were covered in a warm tile or carpeted. Rarely was there anything sharp left where someone could step on it.

But none of that was the point. The shoes were hers. They had been stolen. The woman's situation might be desperate, but that gave her no right to steal. There were things, programs, assistance available if she wanted to use it. Of course, there was a cost. She'd have to wait in line and she'd have to obey some rules. To some any rules were too many regardless of the rewards.

Daily reached out and tugged on the laces of the right shoe. The woman jerked suddenly, drew her feet up, and screamed, "What the fuck are you doing?"

"Taking back my property."

"They're mine now, bitch."

Daily backed off and stood, moving so that she was no longer silhouetted in the hatch. "Not if you can't keep them."

"I'll keep them."

Daily hesitated. All her police training had taught her to try to defuse the situation. Talk and negotiate and persuade. But this was something new and different. It wasn't cop to perpetrator. It was one woman to another. A thief to the victim. Talking would do no good. The woman thought that she was corridor smart while Daily was a neophyte who didn't understand the situation and wasn't tough enough to defend herself.

There was one other thing that Daily knew. Brackett had told her a dozen times if there was nothing else to be done, if there was going to be a fight and you knew that it couldn't be avoided, then the only intelligent thing to do was get in the first punch.

Keeping her eyes on the other woman, Daily advanced slowly, tentatively. Her opponent grinned as if sucking Daily into a trap, but before it could be sprung, Daily attacked. She kicked once, driving her foot into the pit of the woman's stomach. The blow caught her completely by surprise. She fell back, bounced off the bulkhead, and dropped to the deck doubled up and trying to breathe.

Daily slipped to her knees and began tugging at the shoes. She pulled one free and was working on the other when the woman struck back. She kicked, but the flash of movement was enough to alert Daily. She twisted and ducked and the kick bounced off the point of her shoulder, deadening her left arm.

She had forgotten the other advice that Brackett had given her. Once the opponent is down, don't give her a chance to get up again.

Falling back, she rolled and came up on her feet. The woman was up too, facing her, but now she was ready. She held her hands up and her eyes were locked on Daily.

"Pretty good but I'm ready now."

Daily backed up and then stopped. "They're my shoes. Give them to me."

"Take them."

Daily stepped forward, kicked, and then fell back. The woman attacked, swinging her fists. She stomped on Daily's toes and then connected with a fist. Daily felt blood from her flattened nose splash over her chin and down her chest. She ignored it, knowing that the damage wasn't bad.

It gave confidence to the woman. She laughed and said, "You're bleeding. Ruining your clothes."

Daily attacked then. She feinted with a kick and used the side of her hand. She then struck with an elbow and caught the woman on the side of the face. As she staggered back, Daily moved in, kicking and punching, driving the woman to the deck. Then, crouching over her, blood dripping on the face of the opponent, Daily watched to see what she would do.

"Now," said Daily, breathing heavily, "I'll take my shoes." She pulled the second one free, picked up the other, and walked into the corridor.

There had been no point to fighting over the shoes. Neither could eat them. Neither needed them to prevent injury. It was one person asserting her authority over another. It was one person establishing herself as the top dog, the fastest gun in the West, and the meanest son of a bitch in the valley. All for no reason.

Shaking her head, she walked down the corridor. She pinched her nose with her free hand, but the bleeding had slowed. Her nose felt like it was packed with something wet and slimy and she had to breathe through her mouth.

But she had her shoes back and she didn't think anyone would ever try to take them away from her again. She had learned something that all the sociological and psychological texts had failed to teach her. Sometimes violence was the only way to solve a problem. Maybe not often and maybe only with violent people, but sometimes it was the only way.

• • •

They took the lift to the lowest level and then stepped out. Obo looked up and down the corridor and asked, in his clipped British fashion, "Which way, old boy?"

"Lower. Toward the stairs. And then down."

"Of course."

Obo led the way, searching the dark corners and crannies off to the right and left. They reached the stairs and found the first of the corridor dwellers. He was sitting on the top step, leaning forward with elbows on his knees. He didn't look up when Obo and Brackett entered. He said nothing to them.

They descended to the next level and exited, walking along that corridor. Now they were finding more people, some sitting and some lying. There were quiet conversations and there were three people sharing a bottle.

They walked on until they came to the end of the corridor, turned, and headed along the next one. Halfway down it they saw a figure standing in front of the lift.

"Sergeant Jennifer," said Obo, forgetting that he had long ago learned that it was proper to refer to her as Sergeant Daily.

"Looks like," said Brackett. He lifted a hand and called, "Jenny?"

When she turned, he could see the bright red of her blood on her face and shirt. "Come on, Obo."

They ran down the corridor but Daily didn't move. She stood waiting for them. She leaned against the bulkhead as if she was suddenly tired.

As Brackett reached her, he asked, "You okay?"

"Bloody nose is all. Just a bloody nose."

"What happened?"

"Woman stole my shoes and I took them back."

Brackett grinned at her. "Good for you."

She shook her head tiredly. She wiped her nose, looked at the blood smeared on her hand, and said, "You wouldn't believe it down here. You just won't believe it."

"Let's get you back up above. You want to see a doctor?"

"I don't need a doctor. I just need to lay down. Wash my face and lay down."

"You get anything on the killer?"

The lift arrived and the doors slipped open. They entered and Obo pushed the button to take them into the upper levels of the precinct.

"They don't even know it's happened," said Daily. "They're so busy preying on each other and stealing from each other that they don't know it's happening."

"It was a long shot at best."

"Sure, Loot."

15 | When All Else Fails, Blame Those With No Political Power

Brackett ordered Daily to remain in her cabin until the doctor cleared her for duty. Her injuries weren't life threatening, unless the bleeding didn't stop and she managed to drown in her own blood. He wasn't worried about it, but there was no reason for her to be involved in the latest activity. Carnes didn't care who completed the mission as long as it was completed.

After leaving Daily, Obo and Brackett went to the main gym where Sergeant Harris, the officer in charge of riot suppression, had assembled his force. They were decked out in riot gear including their nonlethal stun batons, plastic helmets with clear face shields, body armor that would stop a knife blade, a bullet, or absorb the energy of a laser, and leather boots with steel toes and supports. Going up against an unarmed mob, even if they were outnumbered fifteen or twenty to one wasn't dangerous for them.

As Brackett entered, Harris said, "I have gear set aside for you, sir. I'm afraid I've nothing that'll fit the Tau."

"Obo, you can remain here to coordinate and for liaison with Captain Carnes."

"I don't know, old biddy," he said. "Seems that I'll be missing most of the action."

"Unless Carnes gets nasty. Then it'll all be directed toward you."

"I'll strive to do my best."

"Thanks."

"If you'll come with me," said Harris.

He led Brackett across the deck and into the locker room. Extra riot gear was spread out on a long, low table. There were two other men there, supply personnel whose job it was to make sure that none of the gear disappeared.

"Take what you need. I have kickoff scheduled for twenty-two minutes from now. We'll ride down using all the lifts so that no one can escape."

"Sergeant," said Brackett as he sat down to take off his shoes, "you realize that these people have done nothing wrong. Really wrong."

"I thought one of them was a cold-blooded killer."

"We don't know that. All we know is that we've got to clear the people out of there. We need to identify every one of them and get them into the computer. But that is all. I don't want people hurt."

"Yes, sir."

Brackett kicked his shoes away and put on the special boots. He stood and sorted through the helmets, looking for one in his size.

"We don't take any crap from these people," said Brackett. "I want your people to understand that. If anyone gives you any shit, use the stunner."

"Naturally."

Brackett sorted through the vests, found one to his liking, and opened his jumpsuit, sliding it from his shoulders. He donned the vest and then fastened the front of his clothes. Picking up a stunner and checking the charge, he nodded.

"That's got it."

"You want to speak to the troops, Loot?"

"Nah. It's your operation. I'm there to make Carnes happy and keep the brass off your ass."

"I appreciate that."

They returned to the main part of the gym where the troops waited. They were milling around, talking among themselves. A few were drinking coffee and some had other beverages. The mix of men and women was nearly equal.

Harris moved toward the front and raised his voice slightly. "People, we have a jump-off in about seven minutes. Lieutenant Brackett is here as an observer and liaison with the brass. We need to get ID on everyone below and get them the hell out of there. Briefing packages are in the mini computers held by the squad leaders. All contingencies should be covered but I'll be on radio link for clarification. Questions?"

There were none. They all had done this a hundred times in the past, though it had been on planets and not on the precinct. But the rules were the same and the tactics were the same. Don't allow the people to congregate, don't allow them to get behind you, and don't allow them to take the initiative. Keep them off balance.

"Squad leaders, you have your lift assignments. Get your people moving in that direction."

The squad leaders turned and began issuing the orders, but unlike their military counterparts, they didn't scream. They spoke in normal tones of voice and the men and women began to file out of the gym.

Harris moved closer to Brackett. "Do you want to come with me?"

"Sure."

They left the gym and walked down the corridor. Unlike those far below, this one was brightly lighted and painted in a soft, restful, light green. There were no pipes or bundles of cable running along it. Those were concealed in the bulkheads where they wouldn't be seen. Access to them was a little more difficult, but no one complained.

They reached the far lift and waited with a small group of riot officers. There was no talking now. The mission had begun and each of the cops was thinking quietly. No laughing about kicking ass and taking names. They weren't sure what they faced but they faced it with grim determination.

"They're good people," said Harris.

"No doubt."

The doors slipped open and the people entered. The squad leader reached for the buttons and hesitated. Looking at Harris, he asked, "Are you going all the way down with us?"

"If you don't mind."

"Fine."

He hit the button, the door slid closed quietly, and they began the trip.

Sergeant Elizabeth Walsh, known as Liz to her friends and colleagues, was not the best choice for a surveillance mission because she had rarely followed anyone. But Brackett had requested her services and since he didn't tell her to find someone else, she decided to do it herself. It would make her feel as if she was really a Star Cop and not an administrator who never ventured into the field.

Walsh left word that she had an assignment and checked out of her office so that she could change clothes. The file she had pulled about Linda Pierson didn't tell her much, other than the woman was young, had roomed with Susan Sarah Bakker, and that her job was in the support section. Her schooling was listed, as was a little about her family background and her home world. If Walsh wanted more, she'd have to call up the personnel records and that required a number of permissions, and a notice to the one being investigated.

In her own cabin, Walsh changed from her uniform into a dress with a short skirt. She put on comfortable shoes figuring that Pierson would be heading to one of the many clubs if she left her cabin. Then, it was just a question of following her and establishing a way to make contact without making her suspicious. That was a task that was easier said than done, given the layout of the ship and the fact a person couldn't loiter in a corridor the way an operative could to stake out a residence on a planet. There just were no plausible reasons for someone to be standing around a corridor for five, six, or ten hours.

She found the deck that housed Pierson's cabin and walked along it until she came to the right number but rather than knock, she continued on. She reached the end of the corridor but didn't use the end-lift. Instead she stopped for a moment and watched, waiting.

If luck was with her, Pierson would appear in a moment, but there was no reason to suspect she'd have the luck. Without anyone in the corridor, she could stand waiting, but the instant someone appeared, she'd have to leave her post.

And then she got the luck. Pierson exited her cabin, stopped just outside the hatch to pull at the strap on the rear of her shoe and then tug at her hose. As she turned to search the corridor, Walsh slipped back, out of sight, and as she walked toward the lift, Walsh started after her.

There was no cute way to figure out where she was going except to get into the lift with her. As the doors began to close, and Walsh still fifteen feet away, she called, "Can you hold it please."

The doors opened again, and Walsh leapt in. Breathlessly she said, "Thanks."

"Where you going?"

Walsh glanced at the panel, saw which button was lit, and said, "That's good for me."

They rode in silence for a moment and then Walsh said, "Haven't seen you around before."

"Been here for six months."

"Really? I must stay in my cabin too much. Have to get out more and meet the neighbors."

The lift stopped and the doors opened. Pierson stepped out, thought about it, and then said, "See you."

"Right."

As they walked down the corridor, Walsh let Pierson's faster gait increase the distance between them. She looked into the windows of a couple of the pubs as if she was interested in entering, but didn't instead. She followed Pierson, letting her get farther ahead. Pierson finally turned into the Cat's Paw.

Walsh walked to that pub and stopped outside, letting the beat of the music vibrate in the souls of her feet as the sound reverberated through the deck. The round windows were of smoked glass with bright neon in them telling everyone that the place was open.

Walsh stepped to the hatch and then entered. She stopped and searched the crowd until she spotted Pierson sitting at the bar, a drink in front of her already, a man standing next to her, and looking as if she'd been there for an hour. Walsh found a table near the door that had been vacated and sat down using the empty bottles and glasses as part of her camouflage.

By staring at the area behind the bar she realized that she could watch Pierson without it being obvious. Pierson was engaged in animated conversation with the man. He'd leaned down, his ear next to her lips. The music was loud enough to make it difficult to hear anything but the rock and roll.

Pierson picked up her drink, sipped at it, and returned it to the bar. She lifted a hand and the man took it as she spun on the stool. As she slipped to the deck, her skirt rode up giving a good view of her thighs.

The two of them danced to the fast music, swayed together through a slow song, and then the man escorted her back to the bar. He bowed at her once before turning to leave. Walsh didn't recognize him but tried to memorize his face in case it was important.

At the bar, Pierson finished her drink quickly, and then headed for the door. She didn't hesitate for a moment. Walsh was right behind her as she hurried toward the lift.

The meeting had all the earmarks of a rendezvous for some reason other than a quick dance. All that was the cover for something else. Walsh realized that she hadn't been watching as closely as she should have. Pierson could have passed something to the man, or he could have passed it to her. Walsh, not wanting them to spot her, had tried to be casual in her observation and had let too much slide by. It explained why she was in administration and not fieldwork.

In the corridor outside the bar, she saw the retreating back of Pierson as she headed for the lift. Looking over her shoulder, she saw the man walking in the other direction. Walsh, in that moment, understood police work. She knew who Pierson was, and where she was probably going, but she knew nothing about the man. The man was the mystery that needed to be solved. She turned and began walking after him.

The last person that Kimball expected to see in the labs was Carnes. In twenty years, as far as Kimball knew, Carnes had never bothered to come down. It didn't matter what was going on, Carnes found an excuse not to be there. Now, suddenly, Carnes was right there, at the door to his office.

Waving a hand to signal Carnes that he should enter, Kimball asked, "What can I do for you?"

Carnes didn't enter. He stood just outside the office and leaned forward. "I'd like to have the Steelman tapes."

"Copies haven't been made of all of them."

"I don't want copies. I want the originals."

"I can't let them out of my hands without a release signed by a senior administrator."

Carnes smiled. "Like me?"

"Well, yes, I guess so."

"I've got a group who wants to review the Steelman. Psychologists and sociologists. Maybe we can make something from them."

Kimball stood up and said, "We haven't made duplicates of them yet. If you could wait about four hours . . ."

"They're waiting now."

"This isn't right," said Kimball. "If anything happens to the tapes, they're lost for good."

"What do you expect to happen to them?"

"I don't know, but when we depart from established procedure we end up in trouble."

"I'll give you the written receipts so that you'll be covered in any event."

"Then I guess you can have them."

Carnes pulled a document from his pocket and handed it to Kimball. "That should cover it."

Kimball took it but didn't look at it. He tossed it to his desk. "Come on and I'll get you those tapes."

"Thanks."

16 | Jail-House Lawyers Are Never Worth the Price

The plan had been coordinated in the gym with the timing to be initiated with a single, short radio message. Harris let the squad leader spread the troops out along the corridor and then requested that all the other squad leaders report when ready to comply. As soon as he got the word, Harris pointed at the squad leader and the advance began.

The first few men entered cabins on either side of the corridor. They reappeared on one side immediately as those behind leapfrogged forward to invade the next hiding space. On the other side there was a hesitation of only a few moments and then three civilians stumbled into the corridor.

One of the men, dressed in dirty clothes and looking as if he had just been awakened, yelled, "What in the hell is going on here?"

Harris responded, "You are required to return to the upper levels of the precinct."

"My home is down here."

Harris snapped his fingers and pointed at the man. Two Star Cops moved toward the man.

"Oh, no, you don't," he said.

"Don't make it any harder on yourself than it has to be," said Harris, moving toward the man.

The other two, a man and a woman, looking more confused than angry walked toward the police lines. They were passed to the rear without anyone paying much attention to them. One officer, assigned to watch the rear and the lift, had them sit down near the lift.

The lone man stopped near Harris. "I'm going to protest this to the highest levels."

"Feel free to do so but for now you're going to obey our orders."

The man glowered for a moment and then whirled, heading to where his friends waited.

"We need to get someone down here to begin the process of fingerprinting and identification," said Brackett.

"Teams are being formed and will be getting here shortly. Sergeant Wells is in charge there. She'll make sure that everyone found will be logged into the computer."

"Good."

Now the people began appearing in a steady stream. Few of them protested, walking toward the holding area and finding a place to stretch out there. They then went back to sleep or started talking to one another in low tones. No one seemed too concerned about the events taking place around them.

Brackett walked down the corridor and caught up with the teams clearing the cabins. He stopped outside one as the officers entered, the lights flaring suddenly. The two men inside leapt up and without thinking attacked.

The first officer ducked under the fist and used his stunner, striking the man in the center of the chest. The man leapt back, hit the bulkhead, and slid to the floor, a hand clutching his breast.

The second man hit the officer in the side of the neck that was unprotected. He fell to the right, dropping his stunner. He tried to roll away from the man.

The second officer jumped forward and as the man bent to retrieve the stunner, he struck. He touched the base of the man's spine and he dropped to the deck, his face bouncing on the hard metal.

The first officer rolled to his back and sat up. Reaching out, he picked up his stunner. "Fucker caught me on my blind side."

"They're down now."

Brackett asked from the hatch, "You two okay?"

"Yes, sir. We're fine. We'll get these guys taken back to the holding area."

"I want them arrested for assaulting an officer. They can scream and shout, but if they attack, they get cell time."

"Yes, sir."

Brackett retreated and found Harris. "We're going to have to get someone down here to take people up to the holding cells."

Harris lifted a small radio to his lips and made a call. "Got a couple of jailers coming down now. I'll coordinate with the other squad leaders."

"Let them know that we're not going to take any crap off these people."

"Of course."

Brackett stepped back, away from the front of the police line. He leaned against the bulkhead, his arms folded, as the officers moved into more of the cabins. The corridor was filling with the people being turned out. The numbers grew alarmingly and Brackett was surprised that there were so many who weren't accounted for by the computers, rosters, and normal checks of the precinct.

A cop tumbled from a cabin, tossing his stunner into the air. He scrambled to his feet, bent and grabbed his stunner, and leapt back through the hatch. There was a sudden scream cut short and two cops dragged a man out, dropping him to the deck faceup.

"This one resisted arrest."

Brackett moved toward the prone man and looked down into the face. It was a young man, the skin of the face drawn taut, giving the head the look of a skull. Black smudges under the eyes added to the effect. Brackett knew it was the beginning of the end for those addicted to the drug.

The first of the cops had reached the far end of the corridor and had stopped. They turned and looked back at the trail they had cut. There were a dozen people standing in their wake, others sitting on the deck, and a few sprawled where they'd had to use the stunners.

Harris walked to Brackett. "Looks like we've got this area cleared."

"Reports from the other squad leaders?"

"No trouble at all. Little resistance." He grinned broadly. "Stunners sure sap the strength of the troublemakers."

"Right." Brackett watched as the jailers arrived and began moving among people. They used plasti-cuffs on those who'd resisted, cuffing their hands behind them.

Brackett tired of watching and began to search through the vacated cabins, alcoves, and hiding places. There were dozens of places that a knife could be hidden, if the killer wanted to hide it. The smart thing would be to throw it away, drop it into one of the recycling bins so that it would be broken down into its base components and then re-formed into something else.

Two other officers joined him, poking into the dark areas, searching behind grates and equipment and pulling fixtures from the bulkheads.

"You really think we'll find something, Loot?" asked one of the officers.

Brackett, who was crouched near an air return duct, rocked back on his heels and studied the other two men. "I think that we've got to look. To be honest, I think that the killer, if he's down here, will have gotten rid of his weapon. And even if we do find it, there might be no way to tie it to the murders. But we've got to look."

"Yes, sir."

Brackett reached into the duct and felt around. His fingers touched something and he grabbed it, pulling it out. But it wasn't the murder weapon. It wasn't a weapon of any kind. A bottle in a brown bag that held a small amount of liquid. Brackett had found someone's stash. It told him that the people who occupied the level hid things in the ducts but that was all it told him.

"This is going to take weeks," said one of the men. "There

are thousands of hiding places . . . and it doesn't even have to be down here."

Brackett stood and moved along the bulkhead, his fingers following a pipe that was about waist high. There was nothing hidden behind it.

He realized that the man was right. They could spend a week on that corridor and still overlook the weapon if it was hidden there. It was useless to continue the search and Brackett knew it. They could go through the motions to satisfy the brass topside, or he could cancel the search and hope that the killer, if he was among those rounded up, would confess the crime and tell where the weapon was hidden.

"Okay," said Brackett, "let's secure the search. It's not going to do us any good. Join the rest of the squad."

"Yes, sir."

Brackett left the cabin and saw Harris rushing toward him, a hand in the air.

"Captain Carnes is on the horn. Wants to talk to you immediately."

Brackett took the radio, lifted it to his lips, and said, "Brackett here."

"How is it going, Lieutenant?"

"We're clearing the lower levels and moving the people into the holding zones. Resistance has been light and sporadic. No problems."

"Fine. Keep me informed."

Brackett handed the radio back to Harris and shook his head. "I'll never understand Carnes. Wants to know what is happening, but wants to conduct his overview from the comfort of his own cabin."

The people had been moved toward the lifts, surrounded by the jailers. No one was left in the corridor now except for police officers in riot gear.

"We're ready to move lower," said Harris.

Brackett shook his head. He knew that the plan was useless. No reason to continue because this would not identify the killer, or killers, he had to remind himself. It would just shift the problem from one area to another.

"Lieutenant?"

"This is your operation, Sergeant. If you are satisfied with the sweep here, then move lower."

"Yes, sir."

"Progress in the other corridors?"

"They've either reached the end or about to and are waiting for word to proceed."

"Then go."

Walsh followed the man as he entered another tavern, searched among the crowd, talked to one or two people, and then exited. Walsh was able to watch the transactions easily. No one was paying any attention to her. No one cared that she was there. When the man finished his business, he left without ever looking around. It was as if he believed he was invisible.

He left the corridor, taking one of the escalators down. Walsh waited at the top, let him reach the bottom, and then hurried down after him. She watched as he walked to the far end and then whirled, looking at the corridor behind him.

Walsh hesitated only an instant and kept right on walking as if she knew where she was going. The man studied her for a moment, smiled at her, and then turned around again.

Walsh found an open storage area and dodged into it for a moment. She pulled off the short jacket she wore, looked at the lining and decided that there was no way to reverse it. She dropped it to the deck. She grabbed at her hair, pulled it up, on top of her head, and took a clip from her pocket and pinned it up. She had some glasses and she donned them. The disguise wasn't much and if the man got a good look at her, he'd know that she was following him. If he penetrated the disguise, he'd know that she'd tried to fool him.

Peeking around the corner, she saw that the corridor was now vacant. She'd waited too long and the man had escaped, making her look bad.

She stepped out and hurried forward, working her way to the lift at the far end. But before she reached it, she heard a babble of voices from a cabin and stopped, putting her ear against the metal of the hatch. It opened abruptly and Walsh stood staring into an unauthorized laboratory and a rubber-aproned chemist.

"You following me?" asked the man.

Walsh stood for a moment, not sure what to do. She hadn't thought about being caught. And then she knew exactly how to handle it.

"Yeah. I saw you pass a little to the girl in the Cat's Paw."

"You know her?"

"Linda Pierson."

"She know you?"

"Yeah," said Walsh, pushing the bluff as far as she possibly could.

"We go up there, she'll be able to tell me your name and will vouch for you?"

Walsh grinned broadly, showing her perfect, white teeth. At that moment she knew that she'd won because no matter what the man did, she'd be safe. She knew that they wouldn't be checking on her story.

"She'll vouch for me."

"What do you want?"

"The same you gave Linda."

"I didn't give Linda anything. If you knew her, you'd know that."

"Then you gave it to Susan and I want the same. I know that she had some."

"Sell her some of the shit and get her the hell out of here," said a voice in the back.

"How much money you got?"

Walsh dug in the pocket of her skirt and showed him a wad of cash.

"That's enough," said the man.

Walsh pulled it back, holding it against her breast. "I like to know who I'm dealing with."

"Names aren't important . . . unless you're a cop."

Walsh tried her prettiest smile. "Me? A cop? You have to be kidding."

"Now that you have denied that you're a cop, you have lied to me and any evidence you gain will not be admissible if we're arrested."

Walsh knew that his statement wasn't true, especially concerning illegal activities on the precinct itself, but she wasn't going to say that. Instead, she nodded and said, "I'm not a cop." If that made the man more comfortable, thinking that she wasn't a cop, then she wasn't above lying to him. She held the bundle of bills out to him.

The man took them, counted them, returned some of them, and then turned toward his partner. He pushed some powder into a small clear plastic bag. "I didn't measure it," he said. "First-time customers get a generous supply. Next time we'll weigh it carefully.

Walsh took the bag, which she now considered evidence, tucked it away under her blouse, and left. She knew where the lab was, had gotten a very good look at the man and his partner who was obviously a chemist, and knew that she could locate them again. Her job was done.

17 | Sometimes You Have to Force People to Take the Help

Carnes took the Steelman tapes, and although he'd told Kimball that there was a meeting where the tapes were needed, he had lied about it. There was no meeting. Carnes just wanted to review the tapes himself, to see exactly what they showed and to see how dangerous they were to the killer.

He plugged a tape into the player but didn't turn it on. Instead he surveyed the lab to make sure that he was still alone. Satisfied that no one was there, he locked the hatch and then sat down at the controls. He punched up the tape, put it on the main screen, and then watched it as it flickered and flashed, finally stabilizing into a slate gray that contained nothing that was distinguishable as human.

"Great," he said out loud. "Just great."

Leaning to the right, he twisted a knob, touched two buttons, and saw a shape grow out of the mist. He sat back and watched, but nothing happened to it. It stood there and then seemed to bend over slightly.

And then the picture cleared a little and another shape, the second killer, appeared at the periphery of the victim's vision. It wasn't a clear picture, not enough to recognize the killer easily. Study of the tape might lead somewhere, eventually, if the technicians spent enough time on it but Carnes didn't think it would.

He pulled that tape from the machine and inserted the second. It was even worse than the first. The slate of gray was more charcoal than anything else. A shape, it could have been human, moved slowly and then the whole thing turned black as the victim's last remnants and consciousness disappeared.

"Useless," said Carnes.

He pulled it out and jammed another in, but this one was the worst yet. A dark shape seemed to be drawn, holding back the brightness. A shadow moved and then faded. Carnes watched the whole tape.

The last one was better, but there was still nothing on it that gave a real clue to the killers. There were two shadows moving but there was no way to tell anything else. The killers could have been women, men, or something other than human.

Carnes pulled the tape from the machine and stacked them up. He picked them up and walked across the cabin to set them near the degaussing heads. He reached over and turned it on. He stepped back and watched for a moment.

He picked the top tape up and walked back to the player. He inserted it, turned it on, and saw nothing but snow. The tape had been wiped clean.

The bleeding had stopped completely and Daily carefully blew her nose, trying to clean some of the dried blood out. She used her handkerchief carefully and finally could breathe almost normally. She bent closer to the mirror and looked at herself. Her nose was swollen, her eyes were beginning to blacken, and there was dried blood on her blouse.

"Looks like I've been beaten to a pulp."

She stripped her blouse and dropped it on the deck. She grabbed a towel and headed toward the shower. There, she peeled off the rest of her clothes and turned on the water, stepping in. She got herself wet, used her soap, and then rinsed. The water and soap had turned pink from the blood.

She returned to her cabin and dressed again. She knew that she could stay there, sleep if she wanted, but she was too keyed up for that. Her mind kept churning, thinking of what she had seen and done. She relived the fights, seeing them in detail, moving through them in slow motion. She closed her eyes and tried to relax, but just couldn't do it. Too much to think about.

"Okay," she said. "Maybe a little work."

She left her cabin and headed toward the office. Brackett had a report due and she had been going to help him, until she had thought up the undercover assignment. If she could find his notes, she might be able to get a good start on it. Brackett hadn't said anything about it since the killings had started, but it was still due. They might not be pressing him with the murders unsolved, but the report would eventually have to be written.

She took the lift on up and walked into Brackett's office. She turned on the computer, watched as the cursor appeared and then the main menu came up. She scanned it but there was nothing to suggest that Brackett had done any work on the report.

Turning in the seat, she searched the top of the desk for any notes that related to the report but found nothing. Instead there was a folder marked COMPUTER ENHANCEMENT.

She opened the folder and looked at the report on top. It detailed the computer techniques used to improve the quality of the photo that had been made from the Steelman tape. It mentioned that there hadn't been much to work with, but they had done the best that they could. There was a series of photos, graded from that which was most likely to reflect the Steelman data to one that was a clear black and white glossy that looked as if a professional photographer had taken it. Daily pulled it from the bottom of the pile. The reliability of it was less than ten percent. Daily didn't recognize the man.

She flipped through the pile of photos. The top one, which was ninety percent accurate, was a muddy picture with the features very hard to see. She studied it. The man looked to be a small man with shiny hair. His nose was slightly pointed and there was something vaguely familiar about the picture.

She held it up to the light, as if that would help her see it better as she turned and twisted it.

"I know this man," she said, but couldn't see enough detail to let her identify the killer. She thought that it was someone she had seen below, thought that it was probably Peabody, but there was something wrong. Peabody wasn't quite right. The identification was close but she couldn't make it.

She took the next in line but that didn't help. The computer had distorted the man's features as it tried to fit everything into the matrix it had created.

She put the picture aside and turned her attention back to the computer, but her attention kept drifting back to the file and the photos. She took them out and arranged them, deciding that those under eighty percent accuracy were useless. She didn't recognize them.

She set the one photo on the desk and then propped it against the computer so that she could see it easily. As she moved around the office, she kept her eyes on it. Something tugged at the back of her mind but she couldn't place it. The picture drew her attention and suggested something to her, but she just couldn't identify it.

Finally she sat down and then reached for the phone. She punched up the computer lab that had produced the enhancements of the photos. Holding one beside her, she asked, "Did you do these?"

"Right. What do you need?"

"They the best you could get?"

"We gave you everything we could considering what we had to work with. Computer discrimination is only so good and then we fall into the realm of guesswork."

"I'm not criticizing," said Daily. "What I wondered was if anyone had thought to compare the best of the work with the precinct's records to produce a series of suspects."

"Certainly. We're preparing the list now, but given the nature of the photo, we are having some difficulty with preparing the list. If we had something better, we'd be able to eliminate more of the population."

"You can take out the women," said Daily.

"Why? I see nothing in the photo that would allow us to make that determination."

"I believe that you have the photo of a man here."

"Based on what?"

That, decided Daily, was a very good question. It was something about the picture, about the way the man stood, or held himself, or the angular nature of the face that suggested it to her. She knew the man and that was what she wanted to say but couldn't. There were too many questions that she couldn't answer.

In the background, she could hear a discussion by two of the computer technicians. One of them was saying, "I told you it was a man."

"Do this," said Daily. "Process the information so that the women are eliminated. If that doesn't produce results, you can always expand the search field to include women."

"I suppose so."

"How soon can I have a list?"

"We've got a partial listing now. Be another two, three hours if we eliminate the women."

"Can you transmit a copy of what you have already?"

The person on the screen turned away for a moment and said, "James, get a copy of the list up to the Star Cops."

"On the way."

Daily nodded. "Thanks. I appreciate it."

"Probably won't do you any good."

"No," said Daily, "but then I'm paid to follow the leads wherever they go."

As she disconnected, she noticed that the information was beginning to flow. She moved toward the receiver and examined the documentation as it poured out. It included the name of the suspect, how closely he matched the profile developed by the computer, his current assignment, and any criminal background that might be relevant.

As the sheets dropped from the slot, she realized what a task it was going to be. The picture was so poor that it matched a large number of people on the precinct. A dozen officers could spend weeks searching through everything. It seemed that there was going to be nothing to do, but chase down every single man and try to find out if he had any reason to want to kill so many people.

"It was a thought," she said.

Brackett and the rest of the riot squads had finished sweeping the lower regions of the precinct. They had dug out every person who lived or hid down there. They had been pushed into the corridors and then taken upward, toward the holding area. It had taken hours, but Brackett was convinced that they had found everyone who had been down there.

Harris, his helmet held in his hand and his hair matted against his skull, said, "That should do it."

"That it should," agreed Brackett.

They walked toward the lift where the majority of the squad had congregated. They were waiting for the lift. Two men sat on the deck and another few leaned against the wall. All looked tired.

"Good job, people," said Brackett.

"That do us any good?" asked one of them.

"There are people who have managed to escape the computers which makes our job harder. They'll get registered now. They'll probably drift right back down here, but we'll have them in the computer so I would say, based on that alone, we did some good down here."

"That's something."

The doors slid open and the squad began to enter. They crowded in so that nobody was left behind.

"Now what?" asked Harris.

"Your end of it is done. Now it's up to the administrators. Get those people registered, logged into the computers, and then begin cross-checking."

"I couldn't believe it," said Harris. "So many people down here."

"Yeah," agreed Brackett.

Harris stuck a hand in his pocket and leaned against the lift's wall. "You'd think that many people would have been noticed."

"I think they work at staying out of sight."

Harris shook his head. "I don't understand it. There is no reason for it."

Brackett stood silently for a moment and wondered if he understood it. There were those whose circumstances had overwhelmed them. Through no fault of their own, they found themselves with no way to earn a living, with the bank telling them that they had to vacate their quarters, with shop owners demanding payment and no way to get food except to beg for it. There were ways of getting out of the cycle, but it meant signing up for programs and loans and assistance and each one of those had rules and regulations to be met. There were people who'd had enough of the rules and regulations and standing in lines waiting for a clerk to condescend to speak to them.

"Maybe it's a conscious choice," said Brackett. "Maybe it's just what they wanted."

"Still . . ."

"The name of the game is survival. They are surviving. Those who want out now have a golden opportunity to get out. They're in the upper levels . . ."

"As criminals," said Harris.

"No, but there is no other way to process that many people quickly."

"How would you feel?" asked Harris.

"The point," said Brackett, "is that we're doing something about it now."

The lift stopped and the doors opened. The squad began to filter out slowly, each of them looking as if they had spent a week fighting through thick jungle. Harris stood, holding the button so that the lift wouldn't try to move.

"That doesn't seem to be the right way to help people. Round them up and force them to take the assistance. Give them no choice in the situation."

"Better than rounding them up and locking them up without any attempt to change the situation."

As the last of the squad exited, Harris let go of the button and then wiped a hand through his sweat-damp hair. "Well, it's done now."

"Right," said Brackett. "It's done now."

18 | Sometimes an Ambush Is the Only Way

Brackett returned to his cabin to clean up and then decided to check on Daily. He called her but she didn't answer. Hoping that she had taken his advice and gone to sleep, he disconnected and then decided to swing by the office. There was always paperwork that had to be completed, reports to be written, and logs to be filled out.

At the lift he found Tate, or rather Tate found him. He was standing there, waiting, a video camera in his hand. He watched Brackett approach suspiciously and then demanded, "How come you didn't tell me about the wholesale roundup of innocent people you were about to perpetrate?"

Brackett couldn't help laughing. "That is the most loaded question I have ever heard."

"Didn't want the media to watch the Gestapo tactics?"

"People," said Brackett evenly, "were illegally inhabiting the lower levels of the precinct. With the sudden rise in crime in that area, we were justified in enforcing the various laws and regulations being violated."

"That's what you fascists always say."

"Tate, you're not going to get cooperation from me, or anyone else, with that sort of attitude. We took a precaution to prevent more murders in that area. If some of the residents were inconvenienced, that is too bad."

"You want to go on the record?"

"Why don't you do this? Why don't you go find Captain

Carnes and ask him. We were carrying out our lawful orders."

"That's what you fascists all say."

"No!" snapped Brackett. "I said lawful orders. If you check, you'll find that we did nothing to violate the law as written and approved by the government. The fascists to which you refer were not obeying lawful orders. Get that straight and get it straight now."

Tate was surprised by the sudden anger. He retreated a step and lifted his camera to his shoulder as if he was about to tape a story.

Brackett raised a hand to block the lens. "I don't want you taping now."

"But . . ."

"No. I want you to get the facts first. Learn exactly what happened."

"I heard that a number of people were put into the hospital by your tactics."

"Those who resisted. But it's interesting that there are always more police officers hurt than there are your innocent lawbreakers. You ever wonder why that is?"

"Loot," said Tate, "I didn't mean to imply . . ."

"But you did. You implied that we acted improperly when we didn't. You implied that we beat up people, putting them in the hospital, when they attacked the officers first. We did a job that needed to be done and we did it lawfully and by the book. There's your story."

Tate tried to change the subject. "What's happening now? Where are you going?"

"To the office," said Brackett tiredly. "To catch up on my paperwork."

"Not much of a story."

"My life is not geared to producing events that translate into stories for you. You interested in a story, go to the holding area and talk to the people who were living below. There's your story."

The lift arrived and both men entered. Tate set his camera

on the deck and reached over to hit the buttons. "It's hard to find stories sometimes."

"Tough."

"Anything new on the search for the killer?"

Brackctt punched the button and then massaged his forehead like he was developing a bone-crushing headache.

"I've been busy with the roundup down below so I haven't heard anything. If you're going to interview Carnes, he'd be the one to ask."

The lift stopped and Brackett began to exit.

"If you hear anything, you'll let me know?" asked Tate.

"You'll be the first."

Brackett let the doors close behind him and walked down the corridor to his office. He stopped at the entrance and then walked on in.

"What are you doing here?" he asked Daily when he saw her sitting at his desk.

"I couldn't rest. Too keyed up. I thought maybe I could get a head start on some of the reports." She turned to face him and touched one of the file folders. "I found something interesting here."

Brackett dropped into the visitor's chair and reached out. "I haven't looked at those yet."

"Computer projections on what our killer might look like," she said.

Brackett opened the folder and looked at the top picture. "I know this guy."

"That's what I said. I've been running a cross-check based on the computer comparison."

"You get anything?"

"Nothing yet."

Brackett closed the folder but held out the top picture. Suddenly he laughed. "You know who this reminds me of. Carnes. Short, thin guy. Reminds me of Carnes."

Daily snapped her fingers. "That's right."

"Computer give you a match?"

"I haven't found it yet."

Brackett scratched his head. "How many did you get?"

"I've scanned about forty so far. The general appearance fits so many people that the computer can't limit it any more than that."

"But Carnes hasn't come up on the computer match?"

"Not yet, but I'm not done."

"The move of the hour," said Brackett, "is to call Kimball and then review the tapes. See if there is anything more that we can get."

"You don't suspect Carnes do you?" asked Daily.

"I'd like to," said Brackett, "and he is on the list of suspects now, simply because of the computer picture . . . but I don't think we need to worry about him."

"We're not going to interview him?"

"You find a sheet of paper in that pile of computer matches and we'll interview him. Solid procedure and if he gives us any shit, we'll wave that in his face."

Daily broke out laughing. "He's going to be one irritated individual."

"Yeah," said Brackett slowly. "And this sort of thing is enough to ruin a career. The brass can't stand even a hint of suspicion without all the others turning on them. No one wants to get splashed with the fallout."

"When do we go see him?"

"As soon as you find the computer match and I talk to Kimball."

"Yes, sir."

Tate was cooling his heels in Carnes's outer office, watching the artificial secretary go about her work. She was typing rapidly, her head turned as she scanned a sheet, putting all the information into a computer. She paid no attention to Tate, now that he was sitting on the couch waiting for Carnes to invite him into the inner office.

The secretary finally stopped typing, turned toward Tate, and flashed the most incredibly white teeth at him. They almost sparkled.

"You may go in now."

Tate picked up his camera and headed toward the hatch as it irised open. Carnes met him there, looking tired, but holding out a hand to be shaken.

"Welcome, Mr. Tate. I'm very busy now so I hope this won't take too long."

Tate set his camera down and shook hands. Watching Carnes carefully, he said, "I understand how busy you are. I just have a couple of questions. You don't mind if I tape this interview, do you?"

Carnes touched his throat, checking the collar of his shirt, and then patted his hair. "No, not at all. Where do you want me to sit?"

Tate, who was now crouched and working to open the legs of his tripod, nodded at the desk. "Back there will be fine. I'll set up over here so that we can get some of the holo in the background. Be a nice shot."

Carnes retreated to his desk, sat down, and then began to clear the top of it.

"No," said Tate. "Leave the clutter there. Shows that you're working hard. Gives the shot a nice flavor and doesn't look staged."

"Of course."

Tate got the camera set on the tripod, looked through it to focus it, and then switched on the auxiliary light. He made sure that there were no shadows across Carnes's face or on the desk and that the color balance was in sync. Satisfied, he pulled a chair around and sat down with the camera looking over his shoulder.

"Okay, Captain," said Tate, "I'm going to ask you first about the murder case that you and your staff are working on. I'll want the latest information, direction of the investigation, and any new leads that have been developed."

"Less the confidential information. There are some areas in which we can't explore."

"Of course. And then I'll want a rundown on the sweep that took place down below."

"Certainly."

Tate turned and touched the camera and checked to make sure that it was recording. He pointed at Carnes and then asked, "What is the status of your investigation?"

"That's a pretty lousy question," said Carnes. "Just ask me what you want to know."

Tate sat back and stared at Carnes. The last thing he needed was a lecture on how to ask his questions from a police official. He didn't want to seem to put words in the man's mouth. He wanted the question to be broad enough that Carnes would feel free to talk about the subject. Sometimes, when it didn't seem that he was too sharp, that he didn't know what he was doing, the subject opened up, spilling more than he thought he was. Tate liked to take advantage of that.

"I just wondered how it was going?"

"Well."

"Specifics?"

"Can't go into that."

Tate turned around and shut off the camera. "Captain, if you don't want to do this, just say so and I'll go find someone else to interview. I don't need this aggravation."

"Then ask some better questions."

Tate turned on the camera and asked, "Do you have any suspects?"

"We're working on that."

"Which means you have nothing."

"That's not what I said. I said that we were working on it and that's what I meant."

"Who are your suspects?"

"I'm not at liberty to discuss that as I'm sure you can understand."

"How many suspects?"

"A few."

"Twenty? Fifty? A hundred?"

"I've answered that question."

Tate nodded and asked, "When do you expect to make an arrest?"

"Soon."

"How soon?"

"When we make our arrest, you'll know."

Tate found the anger burning through him. Carnes was playing a game, and at the moment had the upper hand. He took a deep breath, stood, and adjusted the camera, focusing it on Carnes's face so that it filled the lens. He then adjusted it slightly so that the camera was looking down on Carnes. Finally, he changed the lighting so that it was stark. The shadows now fell on Carnes, making him look ghoulish.

Sitting down again, Tate said, "Captain Carnes, you have now told me that you are working on the case, that you have dozens of suspects, and that you expect an arrest sometime in the future. Since your answers have been vague and unresponsive, I can only conclude that you are no further along now than you were when the first bodies were discovered."

"That's not what I said."

"That's exactly what you said. Do you want to reevaluate that now?"

"We have some very good leads . . ."

"That tell you what?"

"We know that there were two killers."

"Descriptions?"

Carnes hesitated and began to sweat. Tate noticed that and grinned to himself. A man being interviewed who began to sweat always looked guilty of something.

"I'm not at liberty to give out that information."

"Are you looking for two men? Humans? Or a combination."

"Men," said Carnes. "We just don't get many cases of aliens killing humans. Some of it going the other way . . . humans killing other life forms, but nothing the other way. We're looking for two male human killers."

"Do you have names?"

"Not yet."

"Moving along, what was the rationale behind the disruption caused below?"

"The victims of these crimes have been the people living down there. We were removing the potential victims."

"In violation of their rights."

"No," snapped Carnes, losing his temper. His voice rose and he sputtered for a moment, trying to get his thoughts organized. Finally he said, "When they signed on the precinct, whether to serve in a maintenance area, support area, in the commercial zone, or in the police organization, they tacitly agreed to the rules and regulations of this organization."

"Sure."

"We have done nothing illegal. Now, this interview is terminated."

Tate grinned broadly and said, "Thank you for your cooperation, Captain." He stood and moved to the camera.

"That thing off yet?"

"It is now," said Tate.

"I don't appreciate the ambush tactics that you employ. I agreed to an interview, not an interrogation as if I were the criminal here."

"Sorry you feel that way, Captain, but you forced the issue. A little cooperation goes a long way." Tate stopped breaking down the camera and turned to face Carnes.

"I'll remember this," said Carnes. "Don't think that I'll forget this."

"Would you care to go back on the record with your threat?" asked Tate. He pushed the camera around so that it was aimed at the captain.

"That was no threat. That was a promise, mister. You just remember it."

"Sure, Captain," said Tate. "Sure."

19 | Sometimes the Answer Is the Simplest Solution

"Got it," said Daily, holding up the document as if it were a talisman. "Got it."

"Close match?"

"Sixty percent on physical features alone," said Daily. "Knocks it way down in other areas since Carnes is a police official. When all factors are considered, there is a less than 15 percent match."

"Well, in the normal course of an investigation," said Brackett, "we would interview the suspects in order starting with the most likely first, but we'll go talk to Captain Carnes. If nothing else, it'll piss him off."

"Yeah," said Daily.

"No, first I want to talk to Kimball and take another look at the Steelman tapes."

There was a tap at the hatch and Brackett turned, "Come ahead."

Walsh, still dressed as she had been when she had followed first Pierson and then the man, appeared. "Lieutenant, did you want a report?"

"What's this?" asked Daily.

"Sergeant Daily, do you know Sergeant Walsh?"

"We've met," said Walsh.

"I had Walsh watching Linda Pierson." Turning his attention to Walsh, he said, "Let's have it."

"Pierson went back to the Cat's Paw and met with a white male . . ."

"ID?"

"I haven't made it yet, but I will. Anyway, Pierson seemed to buy something from him and then left. I followed the man instead."

"Good."

"Got a location where they're—he met with another man—where they're manufacturing drugs." She pulled the plastic envelope from her pocket. "Got the proof."

For the moment Brackett forgot about questioning Carnes. He leaned forward, took the envelope from Walsh, and then punched a code into the phone.

Obo appeared and said, "Hulloo, old boy."

"Need you in the office as quick as you can get up here," said Brackett.

"On my way."

Disconnecting, Brackett said. "I want you to get that analyzed. Then you, Obo, and another two or three officers raid that cabin and arrest the manufacturers."

"Yes, sir."

Then, thinking about it, Brackett said, "Daily, why don't you get things organized here. That photo, with the update sheet, and we'll then go see Carnes. I'll go up to see Kimball with Walsh here. She can get that analyzed and I'll pick up the Steelman tapes."

"Right."

Brackett and Walsh left his office and took the stern lift to the lab. Kimball was sitting in his office, feet propped up, reading a novel from the screen of his computer.

As they entered, he looked up, waved them forward, and then pointed at the screen. "Western. Old Earth. Unbelievable. Two men walking out to face each other, guns blazing."

"Then why read them?" asked Brackett.

"Why not?"

"Sergeant Walsh here has something that she'd like analyzed."

Kimball dropped his feet to the deck and took the plastic envelope from Walsh. He held it up to his eyes, examined it closely, and announced, "Looks like a sample of that drug we've been having trouble with."

"You put that in writing?" asked Brackett.

"Hell no." Standing, Kimball said, "Not until I run a test or two. You have a few minutes?"

"Sure."

They followed Kimball from this office, through the autopsy room, and into a small lab hidden behind a hatch at the far end. Kimball waved a hand as the lights came up. "Toxicology lab. We can identify, in a matter of minutes, over sixty thousand different compounds, the majority of which, if taken in the proper forms in sufficient quantities, will kill a human. Many of them are nearly impossible to detect, and in the old days, murderers who were clever enough to employ them often got away with their crimes."

Brackett shot a glance at Walsh and said, "I didn't come here for a lecture on the art of murder."

"You should take the tour sometime," said Kimball. "You might learn something."

"Thanks."

Kimball pulled a stool from under a table, set the envelope on the hard, shiny surface of the work station, and said, "This shouldn't take long. We already suspect what it is. Given that, I can limit the test to those that will identify that specific substance and that will give us the purity of the sample."

"Why do I feel like I'm suddenly back in high school chemistry?" asked Brackett.

"I don't know," said Kimball innocently. "Why do you feel that way?"

Brackett ignored the question and watched Kimball work. He took a sample of the material from the envelope, dropped it into a glass test tube, and then added another chemical. He shook the tube to mix the two substances and watched as the powder turned a violent pink.

"You've got yourself some of the synthetic opiate. I'd say the purity is close to one hundred percent. They almost never sell it that pure. First, it could kill quickly if taken in a normal dose, and two, by cutting it, they can increase their profits many times."

Brackett turned to Walsh. "You go have the warrants issued and then arrest the two men you saw, confiscate all their equipment and drugs, and then search their personal quarters and any other properties they frequent."

"Yes, sir."

"I want Obo with you when you go."

"Yes, sir."

"When you've completed that, report to me. I want to know the outcome."

Walsh nodded and headed toward the hatch. She stopped short and turned back. "I'll need a report from you, Dr. Kimball, and I'll need the rest of the sample."

"Almost had you," said Brackett. He handed the envelope to her.

"Report will be down in thirty minutes," said Kimball. "Just a matter of typing the right answers on the short form."

"Thanks."

As she left, Kimball leaned back, elbows on the table. "Nice-looking woman."

"Good thing you didn't say that earlier. She might have taken offense."

"Nothing wrong with appreciating beauty, especially if you do it carefully and treat them with respect."

"She deserves it," said Brackett. "She's a very good cop. Though a little overly enthusiastic, but a good cop."

"Now," said Kimball, "what can I do for you?"

"Need the Steelman tapes from the murder victims. We managed to get a computer match with one of the images. Or rather, about a thousand matches, and I hoped there was something we could do to enhance it a little more."

"Captain Carnes has them."

"Oh?"

"Picked them up for some kind of high-level meeting with the brass about this."

"He checked them out properly?"

"Yeah. I didn't get the copies made yet and he didn't want to wait. But he did give me a receipt for it."

Brackett stood for a moment and scratched his head. Finally he said, "Let's look at that receipt."

"It's on my desk."

"You really should follow procedure," said Brackett. He held up a hand to stop the protest and added, "I know, I know. I'm a great one to talk about procedure, but they're easy to follow and when you use them, the brass can't fault you."

"Until they change the rules."

"Right."

They returned to Kimball's office and he plucked the sheet of paper from the snowdrift that covered his desk. He held it out to Brackett.

Grinning, Brackett said, "This proves nothing."

"What?"

"It's not signed and it doesn't describe the items removed from the lab."

Kimball grabbed it, read it, and then dropped into his chair. "That son of a bitch sandbagged me."

"The real question," said Brackett, "is why a captain would do something like that. Carnes is a stickler for procedure. If the i's aren't dotted, you can expect a call from him."

"That's why I didn't even look at it. He always has the proper forms, filled out properly. Why would he do this?"

"That," said Brackett, "is the question."

Harris stood at the hatchway and looked at the people assembled in the holding area. They were crammed in, standing with little or no room to move. Dozens of them, rounded up by his squads as they had cleared the lower levels of the precinct. Those who had shown a bent toward violence had been arrested and were now in cells awaiting arraignment on a variety of charges. Those who had not protested too much, who had not physically resisted, had been brought here.

"Too many people," said a clerk who had moved closer to Harris. "Way too many."

"Ours is not to reason why," said Harris. "Ours is to plug the data into the computer for the powers that be."

"Yeah. Right."

Police officers, many of them wearing riot gear, moved through the crowd, forcing the detainees into lines so that they could begin the processing. Clerks with computers sat at a dozen tables, and formed the head of the dozen lines.

"Going to take hours," said the clerk.

Harris nodded and then turned, walking away. He found two officers standing at the entrance to the area, more or less guarding it so that the prisoners couldn't, or wouldn't, escape.

"If anyone needs me," he said, "I'll be with Lieutenant Gates for the next fifteen or so minutes."

"We'll hold the fort."

"Thanks." Harris hurried from the area and walked down the corridor until he found Gates's office. The lieutenant was in, sitting behind his desk, watching the progress of the processing on both video and on the computer screen. Harris knocked, and entered when he was waved in.

"Got a question, Loot," said Harris. "We got a lot of people in there who have been living down below."

"Right. I know that. You think that we're going to need more security?"

"Nah," said Harris. "Much simpler than that. These people have been living hand to mouth for weeks, maybe months. Strikes me that if we get sandwiches and drinks up to them, we can pacify them easily. They'll get something for their trouble and we'll be able to control them easier."

"Harris," said Gates, "you worry me. Standard practice would call for adding officers if you suspect trouble. Beat the fuckers into submission."

"Of course, but isn't this easier. We buy their cooperation with a little food and no one gets hurt."

"That's what I mean," said Gates. "Thinking things through and finding a solution that follows the path of the least resistance. I don't know."

"You mean that you're not going to authorize the food?"

Now Gates laughed. "Of course I'm going to authorize it. It's the perfect solution. What else can I do?"

"How soon?"

"You go make the announcement and I'll get the stuff arriving in the next thirty minutes or so."

"Great."

Harris returned to the holding area where it seemed more orderly. The lines had been straightened and separated. Now some of the people sat on the deck while they waited. Others talked quietly among themselves. Those at the very end had stretched out and had gone to sleep. It didn't seem that anyone would be causing any trouble for the clerks.

Harris drifted toward the head of one of the lines and watched as a clerk processed the information. A man sat in a chair, leaning an elbow against the table, resting his head in his hand as he tried to answer the questions. He looked bored with the process but he was cooperating.

"When did you come aboard?" asked the clerk.

"Be two years ago in August. Going to work maintenance on the propulsion system but I got tired of it. Nothing to do but sit around and play cards with the same assholes day after day. Just got tired of it."

"When did you quit?"

"Didn't quit. Just stopped going to work. Then the supervisor started hassling me. Calling the cabin, coming by, asking me to report. Got so that I couldn't get away from him. He'd find me no matter what I did, so I hid from him. Stayed away for a week, or a month, and when I returned to the cabin, someone else was living there."

The clerk sat back and said, "And no one came looking for you?"

"Must of figured it was too much work. Must have gotten me replaced so maybe he didn't care."

Harris moved forward and whispered to the clerk. "Why don't you access the pay records and see when he received his last credit."

The clerk nodded, saved the information he'd typed in, and then cleared the screen. Accessing the mainframe, he typed in the name and number of the man and waited. When the information appeared a moment later, he tapped the screen.

"There. Guy's supervisor is drawing the pay. Now I understand how this guy got lost in the system."

"Make a note of it and we'll go talk to the supervisor in the next few days."

"That'll be interesting."

"Make a note of anything like that. Might explain why some of these people have fallen through the cracks."

"Right."

Harris then walked to the center and raised his voice, announcing that food would be arriving in a few minutes. Those who were hungry could take what they wanted. Processing would proceed as quickly as possible and anyone interested in finding employment, permanent residence, and rejoining the society should let the clerks know.

Satisfied with that, he walked back toward the hatch. He watched the activity for a few moments and then said to the men there, "Looks like everything is going to work out just fine now."

"Unless someone gets really pissed."

"They're getting free food, help if they want it, and we're turning them loose once they've been logged into the computer system. Why would anyone get pissed?"

"Yeah. Why?"

20 | Worrying Is Always the Worst Part

Brackett returned to his office and found that Daily had gotten everything ready to confront Carnes. She was still sitting at his desk, the files all ready. When he entered, she asked, "Is this really a good idea?"

"Of course not," said Brackett. "Going after a member of the brass can always backfire if it's not handled exactly right. We have to be very careful."

"That's not what I meant," said Daily. "You know as well as I that Carnes isn't really a suspect."

Brackett sat down in the visitor's chair and leaned forward, his eyes locked on hers. "Let's say that we got a match on a shopkeeper on the retail level. Let's say that he was a, or rather is, a pillar of the community. Now, would we go talk to him about the match?"

"Yes."

"Carnes is no different. We have to check him out." Brackett laughed. "Rather than check him out later, we're going to do it now. Eliminate him from the running so that we can concentrate on the others."

"Still . . ."

"Then look at it this way. We'll let no hint of favoritism affect our work. Carnes's name came up and rather than whitewash it, we went and talked to him first proving that there is not a double standard here."

"When you put it that way."

Brackett took the report and looked at it again. He scanned it and then studied the picture quickly. "And," he said, "there is one new piece of evidence. Carnes has checked out the Steelman tapes. Or maybe I should say that he took the tapes but didn't check them out."

"Meaning?"

"He gave Kimball a blank form. Kimball didn't look at it since Carnes is a book man and has never done a thing that wasn't in the book."

"That's interesting," said Daily.

"But not conclusive," said Brackett. "I know. But it is an interesting deviation and when we get behavior that is abnormal, we must investigate it."

"You've convinced me," said Daily. "We go see Carnes and ask him about this."

"And when we get the logical answers, we then take the investigation in other directions, warm and happy in the knowledge that we have pursued all our leads in a proper and diligent manner."

They stood and Brackett tucked the file under his arm. He didn't expect Carnes to be pleased with the inquiry. In fact, he expected Carnes to explode into anger that he had even been considered a suspect. Brackett couldn't wait to see his reaction because he knew that Carnes could do nothing about the questioning. It was proper police procedure and if Carnes complained, the brass wouldn't back him.

This is going to be fun, thought Brackett.

Obo, Walsh, and a half-dozen other officers met in Walsh's office. She was wearing a laser guard over her uniform shirt. She had weapons attached to it, including a powerpack to drain the energy of a beamed weapon, if it struck her. Her helmet, made of a wire mesh with a silvered visor to reflect energy, sat on her desk. Although she wore a short skirt, she had on shin guards. It looked as if she were ready to invade another planet.

Obo, in a regulation uniform modified for his larger

frame, stood near the hatch, holding his helmet in his hand. He carried no weapons, figuring that he wouldn't need them on the precinct and besides, everyone else was armed.

The other four, three men and one woman, were attired in the same fashion as Walsh. All were younger officers, and two of them had been assigned to administrative duties after graduation and had not been involved in investigation.

Walsh watched the screen of the computer on her desk, waiting until the final approval for the raid came. The brass hats, in their offices four levels above, were networking the information about drug dealers that Walsh had found.

"Just how are we going to do this?" asked one of the men.

"Obo," said Walsh, "Call up the schematics of that section of the precinct and use the center screen."

When the schematic appeared, Walsh walked to it. "This is the cabin where I saw the drug operation. You'll notice that there is only the single hatch and no ductworks, cat-walks, or other exits available. One officer at one end of the corridor, one at the other in case one of the men escapes. Obo, Arbner, and I will go in to make the arrests."

The others crowded around her and studied the schematic. Walsh looked into the faces of the officers with her. "Any questions?"

"Who goes in first?"

"I will," said Walsh.

"There could be more than two people in there by now. Or no one," said Arbner, the other female officer.

"I doubt they'll leave the cabin unattended because they have their equipment in it. If it is, I can find the two men who were there. No problem."

She moved back and turned her attention to the computer screen. The cursor was flashing at the top left of the screen and then began sprinting across, leaving a trail of letters and words behind it.

"This is it," she said. Then, reading out loud, added, "We're to arrest them, confiscate their equipment and any drugs that we find. Anyone in the cabin will be taken into custody, even if that person has nothing to do with the operation and has yet to purchase, or is not in possession of the drugs. We are cleared to go now."

Walsh picked up her helmet, donned it, and then stepped to the printer where a copy of the arrest warrant was waiting. She picked it up, folded it the long way, and stuck it into her pocket.

"Follow me," she said.

The team left the office and walked to the lift, passing a dozen other officers involved in other activities. They waited for the lift and then entered it when the doors opened.

As they rode lower, Walsh said, "I don't want any shooting if we can help it. We take them quickly and easily and then move them right up to holding for processing. I want this as clean as possible."

"But we can shoot," said Hackworth. He was the youngest of the men, had light blond hair and a round, ruddy face.

"If it is necessary," said Walsh, "but it will only be necessary if we allow the situation to get out of hand."

The lift stopped and the doors popped open again. Walsh reached out and hit the button that would hold the doors open for a moment. Suddenly she was scared—no, not scared, just nervous. Butterflies the size of vultures had launched themselves in her belly. She could feel her knees beginning to shake and wished that she had allowed one of the lieutenants to take over after she had reported what she had seen.

Obo and the others exited and stood waiting. Walsh knew that the die had been cast and there was nothing she could do now. She left and started down the corridor.

"Hackworth, you stay here, close to the lift so that no one can gain access to it."

Hackworth was clearly disappointed but said nothing about that.

They reached the hatch and stopped. Lowering her voice, Walsh said, "Simms, you take your position at the far end of the corridor."

"Right, Sarge."

When Simms reached his position, Walsh said, "I'll go first. Then Obo and finally Arbner. Arbner, you'll have your weapon drawn. We'll both step to the right and you to the left so that you'll have a clear field of fire."

"Understood."

Walsh hesitated and then centered herself in front of the hatch. As it began to iris open, she moved and when she could, she jumped on through, stepping to the right as she'd said she would.

Both men were still inside and they had a couple of customers. The man she had followed earlier turned, recognized her, and grinned. "Back so soon?"

He then realized that she was in a police uniform and that Obo was halfway through the hatch.

"Christ, it's a raid!" yelled the other man.

Now the customers spun. One of them bolted for the door and collided with Obo. He bounced and fell to the deck. Obo dived through and fell on the man.

"You're all under arrest," announced Walsh.

"Bullshit!" said the man. He jumped toward her and took a swing at her chin. Walsh ducked under and kicked out, the toe of her shoe connecting with the man's kneecap. He collapsed, hands around his knee as he screamed in sudden pain.

Another of the customers leapt for the door. She hit Arbner and both of them tumbled back, out of the cabin. Arbner rolled to the right but the customer was faster, gaining her feet. Arbner dived, tried to grab an ankle but missed. The woman fled down the corridor, running right for Simms.

Inside the cabin, Obo was on his feet again. He advanced on the other drug dealer who was trying to pull a knife from inside his waistband. He jerked it free and pointed the blade at Obo's abdomen.

That didn't bother Obo. He advanced slowly, but kept his attention focused on the knife. He watched as the point dipped and whirled. And when the man made a sudden lunge, Obo swatted the knife to the side. The blow connected with the man's wrist and deadened his whole arm. The knife spun off to strike the bulkhead.

Obo swung a huge fist and hit the top of the man's head. His knees buckled and he slumped to the deck without a sound. Obo stepped over the body and turned.

But the fight in the cabin was over. Arbner was centered in the hatch, her weapon out. The remaining customer stood with her hands raised above her head, looking from Walsh to Arbner and then to Obo.

Walsh had rolled the one man to his stomach and cuffed his hands. He still lay on his side, his one knee drawn up with blood staining his pants. He was moaning quietly, his eyes closed.

"That's got it in here," said Walsh. "One got out. You stop her?"

Arbner shook her head. "Got by me but I think Simms has her."

Walsh glanced back and saw that Obo had the situation in hand. She leapt through the hatch and saw that Simms had momentarily caught the woman escapee.

But the scene changed suddenly as the woman whirled and kicked. Simms dodged to the right and hit the bulkhead. He seemed to sag and then jumped forward, grabbing at her. He caught her shoulder and spun her around. She tried to kick again but lost her balance, falling to her back. Simms moved so that he was between her and the empty corridor.

Simms moved toward her and helped her to her feet, moving cautiously in case she attacked again. Together they headed back up the corridor, the woman two or three feet in front of him.

"Got this one."

Walsh nodded and turned to look back in the cabin. Obo had gotten the one man to his feet, but the other was still unconscious on the deck. Arbner had the woman handcuffed and ready to get out.

Hackworth came from the other end of the hallway and stopped short. "We through?"

"Got them," said Walsh. "Let's get the interior cleaned up now."

Together they entered the cabin. Walsh ignored the people for the moment and walked to the worktable. There were canisters filled with powder, there were various measuring devices, beakers, test tubes, and even a device to mix the chemicals quickly and efficiently. To one side was a box filled with plastic envelopes filled with the drug.

"We'll need to get all this tagged and moved up to the property room. Simms, why don't you begin sorting through it."

"Sure, Sarge."

The unconscious man stirred, groaned, and sat up. Obo moved toward him and then cuffed him before lifting him to his feet with ease. "We can take them all to holding now, old girl," he said.

"Arbner, stay with Simms and help him collect the evidence. The rest of us will go on up."

"What if someone shows up to buy something?" asked Arbner.

Grinning, Walsh said, "Sell it to them, get the money in your hands and the drug in theirs, and then arrest them for possession of drugs. That's if they're stupid enough to buy it from you. If not, get their names, assignments, and residence, and we'll talk to them later. We'll be back to help as soon as we get everyone processed."

"Okay."

Walsh stepped into the corridor and waited until all the suspects were lined up, ready to move. She realized then that her butterflies were gone and that she hadn't thought about it from the moment that the hatch had opened. The raid had taken only a minute to accomplish and no police officer was hurt. It had been a success.

As they reached the lift and Hackworth touched the buttons to call for the elevator, Obo said, "Most commendable, Sergeant. A top-notch, ripping exercise."

"Thank you," said Walsh. "I appreciate that."

The lift arrived and the prisoners were loaded on it. The police officers joined them and as the doors closed, Walsh realized that the raid was over. Finally over, and she had something that would look good on her record.

"Yeah!" she said quietly. "Yeah."

21 | Sometimes the Bad Guy Is Right Under Your Nose

Sitting in the outer officer, waiting for Carnes to see them, both Brackett and Daily realized the ridiculous nature of their task. They were about to accuse Carnes of killing a number of drug users in the lower regions of the precinct because he bore a slight resemblance to a tape created from the brain cells of a dead person. Not the best of evidence.

Daily was sitting on the edge of the couch, looking as if she were going to get up and run at any moment. She kept flipping her hair off her forehead and adjusting her shirt as if she were about to appear on the video.

"Maybe we should get out," she said again.

Brackett, trying to look calm, just shook his head and said, "We've been over that. Proper police procedure."

"Sure."

The artificial secretary glanced at them, smiled brightly, and said, "You may go in now."

Brackett stood, adjusted the papers in his folder, and said, "Thank you."

Together they moved to the hatch, let it iris open, and then stepped through. Carnes was sitting behind his massive desk, the holo sun was hanging low over the holo city and bathing the office in a dull orange glow.

Waving a hand at the visitor's chairs, Carnes said absently, "Take a seat. I'll be finished with this in just a couple of moments."

Brackett watched as the artificial sun slipped a little lower and the lights in the holographic buildings started to come on. It was an effective illusion.

Carnes finally finished and pushed his work aside. He sat back, steepled his fingers under his chin, and asked, "Now what is so important that you have to bother me?"

Brackett shot a glance at Daily, grinned at her, and said, "We're working on the slasher murders . . ."

"I know that. I believe that I'm the one who assigned you to them."

Brackett took the photo from the folder and set it on the desk near Carnes. "Computer says that your personal profile fits into the parameters of that Steelman photo."

Carnes sat for a moment and didn't move. His eyes flickered to the photo and then back at Brackett. "You're not seriously suggesting that you have a picture of me?"

Brackett had expected a number of responses but the one he got wasn't one of them. He had expected Carnes to pick up the photo and examine it. He'd expected rage from Carnes that he was even considered. But the indifference wasn't quite right and that bothered him.

"Computer says that it's possible," said Daily. "Gave us a list of people to contact."

Carnes shifted his attention to her, as if appreciating the opportunity to think. "How many are on the list?"

"Fewer than a dozen," said Brackett, interrupting.

"How many have you talked to?"

"You're the first."

"Brackett, you're a smart ass. So are you, Daily. Now get out of here."

"No," said Brackett. "We're here in the course of a legitimate investigation and we will not leave until we've satisfied the requirement. Now, do you have any explanation why the computer would target you as one of the suspects?"

"Don't try those bullshit questions on me," said Carnes. "I know all the tricks. And you know that it will target anyone who fits the profile. Anyone."

"Do you have an alibi for the time of the murders?"

"Hell," said Carnes, "we don't know the exact time of the murders, but you can check my daily logs if it'll make you feel better." His voice had risen slightly but he attempted to remain calm.

Daily asked, "Then you know nothing of the murders."

"Hell, I was one of the investigative officers."

"Any theories as to why the killer wasn't covered in blood?" asked Brackett.

"Coveralls?" said Carnes.

Brackett launched into a series of questions that he didn't expect Carnes to answer. If Carnes was innocent, and there was no real reason to suspect that he wasn't telling the truth, Carnes would have no answers. But even so, Brackett was going to conduct the investigation in a proper fashion, so he continued to shoot the questions. And Carnes continued to answer them but before he finished the answer, Brackett had another one.

Finally he asked, "Why'd you get the Steelman tapes from Kimball?"

"I didn't get those tapes."

"Kimball said you did."

"Kimball is mistaken. Ask him if he can prove that I checked out those tapes."

And in that moment Brackett knew that Carnes was guilty. It hit him like a wet slap in the face. Carnes was the killer. It all revolved around the tapes. Tapes that Carnes had insisted be made and then had checked them out. Kimball had told him that Carnes took them and Carnes had violated procedure by not signing for them.

Brackett kept on pushing, asking more questions, searching for the truth. "Why do you think the killer targets users rather than pushers and manufacturers?"

"Pushers are too hard to pin down. They cover their tracks but the users don't. They're so strung out that they can't think. If you remove the incentive to produce the drugs, then the pushers go away."

Daily said, "We've managed to find a pusher and manufacturer."

"Luck," said Carnes. "Your sergeant just stumbled on it and we didn't give them time to get out."

Brackett stood suddenly and plucked the picture from the desk where Carnes had left it. He stuck it into the folder and said, "We've taken enough of your time, Captain."

"I've only allowed this," said Carnes, "because I understand the necessity of clearing names from the suspect list. Please don't bother me with this again."

"Yes, sir," said Brackett.

Daily started to speak, but Brackett grabbed her and dragged her toward the hatch.

"What the hell is going on?" she sputtered.

"Thank you, Captain," said Brackett as he pushed her through the hatch.

As it irised closed behind them, Daily whirled, ignoring the artificial secretary who was still sitting behind her desk working quietly.

"What in the hell . . . ?"

"Outside," said Brackett. He reached out to take her arm.

"Don't you push me around," she flared. "I want to know what in the hell is going on."

They left the office and stopped in the corridor. Brackett looked back, over his shoulder, but the hatch remained closed tightly.

"I know who killed those people."

"Who? Carnes?"

"Right."

"Don't be stupid . . . why do you think it is Carnes?"

"He took the Steelman tapes from Kimball, gave him a blank receipt, and Carnes is such a stickler for procedure that Kimball didn't even check to see if it was filled out right."

"That doesn't prove . . ."

"No, but then Carnes lied about it. Why lie about it if you're not guilty? Something about the Steelmans scared him enough to take them."

"So now what are we going to do?"

Brackett shook his head. "That's the question that I haven't been able to answer."

Carnes waited until Brackett and Daily were out of his office and then threw the first thing he could grab across the room. The little crystal ball shattered in a satisfying explosion of shards and dust.

"Son of a bitch," he said and stood, walking around his desk. He didn't know where to go or what to do. He sat down in one of the visitor's chairs and then stood again.

"Winston is the weak link," he said to himself. "If they get to Winston, he'll open up like a book."

He walked around his desk and sat down again. He opened the middle drawer and took out his letter opener. That was an anachronism because no one received letters and the little paper mail that arrived was already opened. Shaped like a bayonet used on a rifle of an old Earth army, it looked nothing like a lethal weapon in the conventional sense. Anyone finding it in his desk would think that it was a relic being held for its value as an antique and curiosity.

Slipping it into his pocket, he knew that there were no traces of blood on it. He'd even tested it himself, using Luminol, a chemical that reacted with the proteins in blood causing them to glow a pale blue. He made sure that there was nothing about the bayonet to incriminate him.

He slipped from his office, said nothing to the artificial secretary, and then exited into the corridor, walking slowly, as if he had finished for the day. There was no one visible to see his act.

He reached the mid-lift, hit the button, and then stood, shifting from one foot to the other impatiently. He jammed his thumb into the button, as if that could make the lift respond faster.

"Come on," he said. "Hurry up."

In his mind, he could see Brackett and Daily sitting in the cabin with Winston, talking to him like old friends. Lead him on, con him with their friendly attitudes until he let something slip. Once that happened, the game would be over. Winston would fold up like a house of cards. Winston was too smart for his own good.

The lift arrived and Carnes leapt into it and hit the buttons again, not satisfied with the slow response. He stared up at the surveillance camera and then looked down, at the panel showing the passing of the levels.

The doors opened and Carnes sprang out and then looked around wildly as if he'd been caught doing something that he shouldn't. He walked down the corridor, nodded at two women who left their cabin, and stopped outside that of Winston. There he hesitated because he knew that if Brackett and Daily were in there, the game would be over. But they'd said nothing to indicate they knew of Winston and they had left calmly after asking him only a few questions. His impression was that they were riding him because they had the power to do it. They could get even with him.

He stood for a moment, afraid to act, and afraid not to act. He finally reached out and signaled that he was there. A moment later the door irised open and he stepped through, relieved to find Winston alone, sitting on his bunk half-dressed.

"Afternoon, Captain." He spotted the knife that Carnes had removed from his pocket. "We about to go hunting again."

"Things are heating up."

"Yeah, I thought they might. We took out too many too fast. Should have waited for a planetfall."

"That's old news now," said Carnes. "Anybody been here to talk to you?"

"Nope. Quiet as always. Maintain a low profile and no one will bother you."

"Steelman told them that there were two of us. Couldn't tell them much more than that."

Winston bent over and picked up a shoe. "That won't help them at all."

"What would you say if they came to question you?"

Winston stopped moving and looked at Carnes carefully. "I don't know. Depends on what they ask. But I have no reason to kill those people. Not like you do." He kept his eyes on Carnes, his shoe held in both hands as he prepared to put it on his foot.

"My sister died in the hospital of a drug reaction. Official reports say that."

"Of course they do. But it doesn't say what drug or where she got it. What if someone asks that question?"

"No one will," said Carnes. "No reason to ask that question."

"It's possible . . ."

Carnes moved closer to Winston and stared down at the man who he now hated. Too smart for his own good. Stronger than most everyone on the ship. Thick black hair on his head, chest, back, and arms, making him look brutish. Not the intellect that he was in reality.

"We just put our activities on hold for a few weeks," said Winston, glancing down at his foot so that he could pull on his shoe.

Carnes struck at that moment. He jumped forward and stabbed out, the bayonet slipping into the side of Winston's neck. The man jerked to the right nearly yanking the blade from Carnes's hand. He tried to roll away, but Carnes followed, the weapon held up. When he had the chance, he struck again, slashing at the throat. Blood spurted, spraying the bunk, the bulkheads, the overhead, and Carnes but the captain moved in closer, giving Winston no chance. He stabbed again and again, wounding Winston in the shoulders and head.

Winston pushed Carnes away suddenly and then stood up. He looked at the hatch, as if it would provide sanctuary, but then collapsed, falling forward. He bounced on the deck and didn't move.

Carnes stared at the body, but it was obvious that Winston had died. The only witness to the murders was now dead.

Brackett and Daily might be able to build a superficial circumstantial case but it wouldn't be sufficient to convict or even indict. His career might suffer for a year or two but then everyone would soon forget.

He knelt near the body and checked for a pulse. Winston was dead. Carnes stood and turned, looking at the mirror over the tiny sink in the alcove. There was blood sprayed across his face and on one arm, but he'd remained relatively clean. He could wash it away well enough that he could get to his cabin without raising any eyebows.

Laughing, he started cleaning himself. He had it made. He was going to get away.

Brackett and Daily waited at the far end of the corridor, standing in a small alcove that shielded them from Carnes when he left his office. They watched him hurry to the lift, saw his agitation as he waited, and then used the surveillance system on the precinct to verify his destination.

"We go down there now?" asked Daily.

"I think we'll go speak to the man that Carnes was so all fired up to see."

They headed to the lift and took it down. The doors opened on an empty corridor. They exited and walked slowly toward the man's hatch.

"What if Carnes is still there?"

"Then we'll have an interesting time."

Daily took a position on the far side of the hatch, her back to the bulkhead. Brackett, standing on the other side, touched the button, but there was no response.

Then suddenly the hatch opened and Carnes was standing there, a bloody knife clutched in his hand. "Quick," said Carnes, "get some medical help down here. There's a badly wounded man in here."

Brackett stepped back, away from Carnes. "Put the weapon down."

Carnes looked genuinely surprised. "Oh." He stooped and set it on the deck. "Right."

"Sergeant Daily, call for medics and backup," said Brackett.

Daily moved away from the hatch and made the call from the closest intercom.

Brackett looked into the cabin and saw the dead man lying on the deck. "What happened here?"

"Came down to consult with Winston about an ongoing investigation and found him dead," said Carnes. "He hasn't been dead very long."

Brackett kept his attention focused on Carnes. "This is more than a little suspicious. We just question you about a murder case and then find you standing over the body of another murder victim."

"I told you. I just discovered the body and was about to call it in. Then I saw you on the camera."

"Right."

"Don't take that tone with me," said Carnes. "I'm still your superior officer."

The medical team, along with additional officers, arrived then. One of the medics pushed past them, crouched next to the body, and said, "This guy's had it." He looked up, grinning, as if he'd just made a profound statement.

Without taking his eyes off Carnes, Brackett asked, "You bring a Steelman?"

"Nope but the ME will have it. He's on his way down here now."

Grinning at Carnes, Brackett said, "Then we'll have some answers. How long this guy been dead?"

"Fifteen minutes at most," said the medic.

"Then it'll be like watching a viddrama. Clear and clean and we'll see the killer."

"If you get anything," said Carnes.

Brackett glanced at the dead body. "No traumas to the brain, no evidence of drug use, and less than thirty minutes since the victim died. We'll have the perpetrator named in just a few minutes."

Carnes stepped back, out of the way, and watched as more

police entered the tiny cabin. Finally he said, "I'm going to get out of the way."

But before he could reach the hatch, Brackett stopped him. "Where will you be, Captain?"

"My office. When you finish here, come on up and brief me on what you find."

Daily, who had been standing to the side watching and listening, said, "You're going to let him leave? You can't let him leave."

"You can't stop me," said Carnes, but his voice held no conviction.

"Captain, I'm afraid that we're going to have to go up to the holding area."

"I don't think so."

"Don't make this any harder than it is. It's obvious that you killed this man, have participated in other killings, and have tried to block this investigation from the very beginning. Hell, you've stolen evidence. You are under arrest. Make no mistake about it."

"I'll have your badge," said Carnes.

"If I'm wrong, that you will. Let's go."

The officers around watched the exchange in disbelief. One of the medics had stepped back and fallen onto the bunk. No one spoke or moved.

Brackett followed Carnes out of the cabin. The arrest seemed anticlimactic.

Epilogue | The End of an Era

"Some good came out of this," said Tate, sitting at a table in the Cup and Hole. Behind him was the blackness of space, brightened by a smudge that marked the Milky Way, and a thousand pinpoints of light that marked the suns of ten thousand different planets.

"What?" asked Daily.

"I can't see much of anything good when a cop goes bad," said Brackett. "Creates mistrust of all of us."

"Not a real cop though," said Tate. "An administrator."

"That how everyone looks at it?" asked Brackett.

"The word I get is all positive. They look at how you, meaning the working cops, cleaned up the lower levels and eliminated a real problem. People who needed help got it. And the problem with drugs was eliminated here on the precinct. And, finally, it was the cops, working at their best, who discovered the killer and arrested him without any attempts to hide the truth."

Brackett, watching the stars beyond them, said, "Doesn't make me feel any better."

"Hell, Carnes was an asshole."

"You have to look at the big picture," said Brackett. "How would you have felt if it were your sister."

"What?"

"They got his sister hooked on that shit and it killed her. He was just getting even."

Tate pushed the remains of his breakfast away and said, "You don't believe that."

Brackett shrugged. "I don't know. I just don't like the way this thing came out."

Now Daily spoke. "All victims in this one," she said. "No real criminal. No evil lining up to destroy people. Just victims caught up in the circumstances of the situation that none of them controlled."

"So," said Tate. "Now what?"

Brackett looked at Daily. "Now nothing. There are reports to be written and filed, and the investigation must continue. We have to put together an objective case, a body of evidence to prove what we have found and to prove that we are right. And Carnes will have to be tried."

"What'll happen to him?" asked Tate.

"That's not for me to say," said Brackett. "Personally, I hope he'll get some professional help . . ." He stopped talking, realizing that it wasn't his job to decide that. Someone else would handle it.

"Been a long time since there has been a trial here," said Tate.

"We investigate but prosecution normally is left to the courts on the planets where the crimes were committed," said Daily.

Brackett stood up and said, "I've had enough of this. When you get it decided, let me know."

As Brackett left, Tate said, "I didn't think he liked Carnes."

"He didn't," said Daily. "He just doesn't like to see a police officer fall from grace. No matter who that police officer is."

"They're human too."

"Yeah," said Daily, standing, "but Brackett would prefer that they weren't and that is the problem."

With that she left.